Pervish Myth-Behavior

"Nice of you to drop by, mister!"

That was said by a Pervect, one of six who were blocking our path down the alley.

"Of course, you know this here's what you'd call a toll-alley. You got to pay to use it."

"That's right," one of his cronies chimed in. "We figure what you got in your pockets ought to cover it."

I decided that this would be an excellent time to delegate a problem.

"C'mon Kalvin! Do something!"

"Like what? I told you I'm no good in a fight."

"Well, do SOMETHING! You're supposed to be the Djin!"

"Oh, all right!" he grimaced. "Maybe this will help."

With that, he made a few passes with his hands and . . .

. . . And I was stone-cold sober!

"That's all I can do for you," he shrugged. "At least now you won't have to fight 'em drunk."

MYTH·NOMERS
and
IM·PERVECTIONS

Robert Lynn Asprin

ACE BOOKS, NEW YORK

This Ace Book contains the complete
text of the original trade edition.
It has been completely reset in a typeface
designed for easy reading, and was printed
from new film.

MYTH-NOMERS AND IM-PERVECTIONS

An Ace Book / published by arrangement with
Starblaze Editions of the Donning Company/Publishers

PRINTING HISTORY
Donning edition published 1987
Ace edition / November 1988

ISBN: 0-441-55279-X

Ace Books are published by The Berkley Publishing Group,
200 Madison Avenue, New York, New York 10016.
The name ''Ace'' and the ''A'' logo are
trademarks belonging to Charter Communications, Inc.
PRINTED IN THE UNITED STATES OF AMERICA

10 9 8 7 6 5 4 3 2

Chapter One:

"Nobody's seen it all!"

—MARCO POLO

THOSE OF YOU who have been following my mishaps know me as Skeeve (sometimes Skeeve the Great) and that I grew up in the dimension Klah, which is not the center of culture or progress for our age no matter how generously you look at it. Of course, you also know that since I started chronicling my adventures, I've knocked around a bit and seen a lot of dimensions, so I'm not quite the easily impressed bumpkin I was when I first got into the magik biz. Well, let me tell you, no matter how sophisticated and jaded I thought I had become, nothing I had experienced to date prepared me for the sights that greeted me when I dropped in on the dimension Perv.

The place was huge. Not that it stretched farther than any other place I had been. I mean, a horizon is a horizon. Right? Where it *did* go that other places I had visited hadn't, was up!

None of the tents or stalls I was used to seeing at the Bazaar at Deva were in evidence here. Instead, massive buildings stretched up into the air almost out of sight. Actually, the buildings themselves were plainly in sight. What was almost lost was the sky! Unless one looked straight up, it wasn't visible at all, and even then it was difficult to believe that little strip of brightness so far overhead was really the sky. Perhaps this might have been more impressive if the buildings themselves were pleasanter to look at. Unfortunately, for the most part they had the style and grace of an oversized outhouse . . . and roughly the same degree of cleanliness. I wouldn't have believed that buildings so high could give the impression of being squat, but these did. After a few moments' reflection, I decided it was the dirt.

It looked as if soot and grime had been accumulating in layers on every available surface for generations, give or take a century. I had a flash impression that if the dirt were hosed from the buildings, they would collapse from the loss of support. The image was fascinating and I amused myself with it for a few moments before turning my attention to the other noteworthy feature of the dimension: The People.

Now there are those who would contest whether the denizens of Perv qualified as ''people'' or not, but as a resident of the Bazaar I had gotten into the habit of referring to all intelligent beings as ''people,'' no matter what they looked like or how they used their intelligence. Anyway, whether they were acknowledged as people or not, and whether they were referred to as ''Per-vects'' or ''Per-verts,'' there was no denying there were a lot of them!

Everywhere you looked there were mobs of citizens, all jostling and snarling at each other as they rushed here and there. I had seen crowds at the Big Game that I thought were rowdy and rude, but these teeming throngs won the prize hands down when it came to size *and* rudeness.

The combined effect of the buildings and the crowds

created a mixed impression of the dimension. I couldn't tell if I was attracted or repelled, but overall I felt an almost hypnotic, horrified fascination. I couldn't think of anything I had seen or experienced that was anything like it.

"It looks like Manhattan . . . only more so!"

That came from Massha. She's supposed to be my apprentice . . . though you'd never know it. Not only is she older than me, she's toured the dimensions more than I have. Even though I've never claimed to be a know-it-all, it irritates me when my apprentice knows more than I do.

"I see what you mean," I said, bluffing a little. "At least, as much as we can see from here."

It seemed like a safe statement. We were currently standing in an alley which severely limited our view. Basically, it was something to say without really saying anything.

"Aren't you forgetting something, though, Hot Stuff?" Massha frowned, craning her neck to peer down the street.

So much for bluffing. Now that I had admitted noticing the similarities between Perv and Man-hat-tin . . . wherever *that* was, I was expected to comment on the differences. Well, if there's one thing I learned during my brief stint as a dragon poker player, it's that you don't back out of a bluff halfway through it.

"Give me a minute," I said, making a big show of looking in the same direction Massha was. "I'll get it."

What I was counting on was my apprentice's impatience. I figured she would spill the beans before I had to admit I didn't know what she was talking about. I was right.

"Long word . . . sounds like disguise spell?"

She broke off her examination of the street to shoot me a speculative glance.

"Oh! Yeah. Right."

My residency at the Bazaar had spoiled me. Living at the trading and merchandising hub of the dimensions had gotten me used to seeing beings from numerous dimensions shopping side by side without batting an eye. One tended to forget that in other dimensions, off-world beings were not only an oddity, occasionally they were downright unwelcome.

Of course, Perv was one of those dimensions. What Massha had noticed while I was gawking at the landscape was that we were drawing more than a few hostile glares as passersby noticed us at the mouth of the alley. I had attributed that to two things: the well-known Pervish temperament (which is notoriously foul), and Massha.

While my apprentice is a wonderful person, her appearance is less than pin-up-girl caliber . . . unless you get calendars from the local zoo. To say Massha would look more natural with a few tick-birds walking back and forth on her would be an injustice . . . she's never *tried* to look natural. This goes beyond her stringy orange hair and larger-than-large stature. I mean, anyone who wears green lipstick and turquoise nail polish, not to mention a couple of tattoos of dubious taste, is not trying for the Miss Natural look.

There was a time when I would get upset at people for staring at Massha. She really *is* a wonderful person, even if her taste in clothes and makeup would gag a goat. I finally reached peace with it, however, after she pointed out that she *expected* people to look at her and dressed accordingly.

All of this is simply to explain why it didn't strike me as unusual that people were staring at us. Similarly, Pervish citizens are noted for not liking anyone, and off-worlders in particular, so the lack of warmth in the looks directed at us did not seem noteworthy.

What Massha had reminded me of, though it shouldn't have been necessary, is that we were now on Perv, their home dimension, and instead of an occasional encounter we would be dealing with them almost exclusively. As I said I should have realized it, but after years of hearing about Perv, it was taking a while for it to sink in that I was actually there.

Of course, there was no way we could be mistaken for natives. The locals here had green scales, yellow eyes, and pointed teeth, while Massha and I looked . . . well, normal. In some way, I think it goes to show how unsettling the Pervects look when I say that, by comparison, Massha looks normal.

However, Massha was correct in pointing out that if I hoped to get any degree of cooperation from the locals, I was going to have to utilize a disguise spell to blend with them. Closing my eyes, I got to work.

The disguise spell was one of the first spells I learned, and I've always had complete confidence in it . . . after the first few times I used it, that is. For those who are interested in technical details, it's sort of a blend of illusion and mind control. Simply put, if you can convince yourself that you look different, others will see it as well. That may sound complicated, but it's really very simple and easy to learn. Actors have been using it for centuries. Anyway, it's quite easy, and in no time at all my disguise was in place and I was ready to face Perv as a native.

"Nice work, Spell-slinger," Massha drawled with deceptive casualness. "But there's one minor detail you've overlooked."

This time I knew exactly what she was referring to, but decided to play it dumb. In case you're wondering, yes, this is my normal modus operandi . . . to act dumb when I know what's going on, and knowledgeable when I'm totally in the dark.

"What's that, Massha?" I said, innocently.

"Where's mine?"

There was a lot loaded into those two words, everything

from threats to a plea. This time, however, I wasn't going to be moved. I had given the matter a lot of thought and firmly resolved to stand by my decision.

"You aren't going to need a disguise, Massha. You aren't staying."

"But, Skeeve . . . "

"No!"

"But . . . "

"Look, Massha," I said, facing her directly, "I appreciate your wanting to help, but this is my problem. Aahz is *my* partner, not to mention my mentor and best friend. What's more, it was my thoughtlessness that got him so upset he resigned from the firm and ran away. No matter how you cut it, it's my job to find him and bring him back."

My apprentice regarded me with folded arms and tight lips.

"Agreed," she said.

" . . . So there's no point in your trying to . . . what did you say?"

"I said agreed," she repeated. " . . . As in, I agree it's your job to bring Aahz back!"

That took me by surprise. I had somehow expected more of an argument. Even now, it didn't look to me like she had really given up the fight.

"Well, then . . . "

" . . . And it's my job as your apprentice to tag along and back your moves. By your own logic, Chief, I'm obligated to you the same way you're obligated to Aahz."

It was a good argument, and for a moment I was tempted to let her stay.

"Sorry, Massha," I said finally with real regret, "I can't let you do it."

"But . . . "

" . . . Because you're going to be my stand-in when the

rest of the team takes on Queen Hemlock.''

That stopped her, as I thought it would, and she bit her lip and stared into the distance as I continued.

"It's bad enough that the rest of the crew is going to fight my battle for me, but to have both of us sit it out is unthinkable. They're going to need all the help they can get. Besides, part of the reason for having an apprentice is so that I can be two places at once . . . isn't it?''

I figured that would end the discussion, but I underestimated Massha's determination.

"Okay, then *you* lead the fight against Hemlock and *I'll* fetch the Scaly Wonder.''

I shook my head.

"C'mon, Massha. You know better than that. It was my thoughtlessness that made him leave in the first place. If anyone should, if anyone *can* make him come back it's got to be me.''

She muttered something under her breath that it's probably just as well I didn't hear, but I was pretty sure it wasn't wholehearted agreement. With one problem already at hand from my lack of attentiveness to my associates' moods, I thought it ill-advised to ignore the fact my apprentice was upset.

"Look, can we take a few minutes and discuss what it is that's really bothering you?'' I said. "I'd just as soon we didn't part company on an off note.''

Massha pursed her lips for a few moments, then heaved a great sigh.

"I just don't like the idea of your taking on this chore alone, Skeeve. I know you know more magik than I do, but this is one of the meanest of the known dimensions. I'd feel better if you had a backup is all . . . Even if it's just a mechanic like me. These little toys of mine have helped us out more than once in the past.''

What she was referring to, of course, was her jewelry. Nearly all the magik Massha used was of the gimmick variety . . . magik rings, magik pendants, magik nose studs . . . hence the nickname within the trade of "mechanic." She was, however, polite enough to not stress too hard the fact that her toys were often more effective and reliable than my own "natural" form.

"You're right, Massha, and I'd love to have you along . . . but you're needed more against Hemlock. Before you get too worried, though, just remember I've handled some pretty tough situations in the past."

"Those weren't on Perv and you usually had your partner along to handle the rough stuff," she said bluntly. "You don't even have a D-hopper along."

"I'll get it back from Aahz when I find him. If I'm successful, we'll be along together. If not, I figure he'll give me the D-hopper and set it for Klah just to be rid of me."

" . . . And if you can't find him at all?" Massha gestured pointedly at the crowds on the street. "In case you haven't noticed, this isn't going to be the easiest place to locate someone."

For a change, I was confident when I answered.

"Don't worry about that. I'll find him. I've got a few tricks up my sleeve for that chore. The trick is going to be getting him to change his mind."

"Well, can you at least do one thing? As a favor to your tired old apprentice?"

She tugged a ring off her left pinkie and handed it to me.

"Wear this," she said. "If you haven't shown up by the end of the week, I'll come looking for you. This'll help me locate you if you're still in this dimension . . . or do you want to run the risk of being stranded here?"

The ring fit loosely on my right thumb. Any larger, and I would have had to wear it like a bracelet. Staring at it, a sudden suspicion flitted through my mind.

"What else does it do?"

"Beg pardon?" Massha replied with such innocence I knew I was right.

"You heard me, *apprentice*. What does it do besides provide a beacon?"

"Wellll . . . it *does* monitor your heartbeat and alert me if there's a sudden change in your physical condition, like say if you were injured. If that happens, I might just drop in a little early to see what's wrong."

I wasn't sure I liked that.

"But what if my heartbeat changed for normal reasons . . . like because I met a beautiful girl close up?"

That earned me a bawdy wink.

"In that case, High Roller, I'd want to be here to meet her. Can't have you running around with just *anybody*, can we?"

Before I could think of a suitable reply, she swept me into a bone-crushing hug.

"Take care of yourself, Skeeve," she whispered with sudden ferocity. "Things wouldn't be the same without you."

There was a soft pop in the air, and she was gone. I was alone in Perv, the nastiest of the known dimensions.

Chapter Two:

"They don't make 'em like they used to!"
                                    —H. FORD

ACTUALLY, I WASN'T as worried as you might think I'd be from the situation. Like I'd told Massha, I had an ace up my sleeve . . . and it was a beaut!

A while back, I was part . . . heck, I was the instigator of a plan to force the Mob out of the Bazaar at Deva. I felt it was only fair, since I was the one who had given them access to the Bazaar in the first place, and besides, the Devan Merchants' Association had paid me well to get the Mob off their backs. Of course that was before the Mob hired me to run their interests at the Bazaar, and the Bazaar agreed to give me a house and pay me a percentage of the profits to keep the Mob at bay. Sound confusing? It was . . . a little. Fortunately, Aahz had shown me how the two assignments weren't mutually exclusive and that it *was* ethically possible to collect money from both sides . . . well, possible, anyway. Is it any wonder that I prize his counsel so highly? However, I digress.

During the initial skirmishes of that campaign, I had ac-

quired a litle souvenir that I had almost forgotten about until
I was getting ready for this quest. It wasn't much to look
at, just a small vial with its stopper held in place by a wax
seal, but I figured it just might mean the difference between
success and failure.

I probably could have mentioned it to Massha, but frankly
I was looking forward to taking the credit for having pulled
off this chore by myself. Smirking confidently, I glared
around to be sure I was unobserved, then broke the seal and
removed the stopper.

Now to really appreciate the full impact of this next bit,
you have to realize what I was expecting. Living at the
Bazaar, I had gotten used to some really showy stuff . . .
lightning bolts, balls of fire . . . you know, special effects
like that. It's a tight market, and glitz sells. Anyway, I was
braced for nearly anything, but I was expecting a billowing
cloud of smoke and maybe a thunderclap or a gong for
emphasis.

What I got was a soft pop, the same as you get pulling
a cork out of a bottle of flat soda, and a small puff of vapor
that didn't have enough body to it to make a decent smoke
ring. End of show. Period. *Das ist alles*.

To say I was a little disappointed would be like saying
Deveels dabbled in trade. Understatement to the max. I was
seriously considering whether to throw the bottle away in
disgust or actually try to get a refund out of the Deveel who
sold it to me, when I noticed there was something floating
in the air in front of me.

Actually, I should say it was *someone* floating in the air,
since it was clearly a figure . . . or to be accurate, half a
figure. He was bare to the waist, and possibly beyond. I
couldn't tell because the image faded to invisibility below
his navel. He was wearing a fez low on his forehead so it
hid his eyes, and had his arms folded across his chest. His

arms and torso were pretty muscular, and he might have been impressive . . . if he weren't so small! I had been expecting something between my height and that of a three-story building. What I got would have been maybe six to eight inches high if all of him was visible. As it was, head and torso only measured about three inches. Needless to say, I was underwhelmed. Still, he was all I had and if nothing else, over my various trials and adventures, I had learned to make do with what was available.

"Kalvin?" I said, unsure of the proper form of address.

"Like, man, that's my name. Don't wear it out," the figure replied without emerging from under his hat.

Now, I wasn't sure what our exact relationship was supposed to be, but I was pretty sure this wasn't it, so I tried again.

"Ummm . . . do I have to point out that I am your Master and therefore Ruler of your Destiny?"

"Oh, yeah?"

The figure extended one long finger and used it to push the fez back to a point where he could look at me directly. His eyes were a glowing blood red.

"Do you know what I am?"

The question surprised me, but I rallied gamely.

"Ah, I believe you're a Djin. Specifically a Djin named Kalvin. The Deveel I bought you from said you were the latest thing in Djins."

The little man shook his head.

"Wrong."

"But . . . "

"What I am is drunk as a skunk!"

This last was accompanied by a conspiratorial wink.

"Drunk?!" I echoed.

Kalvin shrugged.

"What do you expect? I crawled into the bottle years

ago. I guess you could say I'm a Djin Rummy.''

Whether my mouth was open from astonishment or to say something, I'm not sure but I finally caught the twinkle in his eye.

''Djin rummy. Cute. This is a gag, right?''

''Right as rain!'' the Djin acknowledged, beaming at me with a disarming smile. ''Had you going for a minute, didn't I?''

I started to nod, but he was still going strong.

''Thought we might as well get started on the right foot. I figure anyone who owns me has got to have a sense of humor. Might as well find out first thing, ya know? Say, what's yer name, anyway?''

He was talking so fast I almost missed the opening. In fact, I would have if he hadn't paused and looked expectantly at me.

''What? Oh! I'm Skeeve. I . . . ''

''Skeeve, huh? Funny name for a Pervert.''

My response was reflexive.

''That's Per-*vect*. And I'm not. I mean, I'm not one.''

The Djin cocked his head and squinted at me.

''Really? You sure look like one. Besides, I've never met anyone who wasn't a Perver . . . excuse me, Pervect . . . who would argue the difference.''

It was sort of a compliment. Anyway, I took it as one. It's always nice to know when your spells are working.

''It's a disguise,'' I said. ''I figured it was the only way to operate on Perv without getting hassled by the natives.''

''Perv!''

Kalvin seemed genuinely upset.

''By the gods, Affendi, what are we doing here?''

''Affendi?''

''Sure. You're the Affendi, I'm the Offender. It's tradition among Djins. But that's beside the point. You haven't answered my question. How did an intelligent lad such as yourself end up in this godforsaken dimension?''

"Do you know Perv? Have you been here before?" I said, my hopes rising for the first time since I opened the bottle.

"No, but I've heard of it. Most Djins I know avoid it like the plague."

So much for getting my hopes up. Still, at least I had Kalvin talking seriously for a change.

"Well, to answer your question, I'm here looking for a friend of mine. He . . . well, you might say he ran away from home, and I want to find him and bring him back. The trouble is, he's . . . a bit upset at the moment."

"A bit upset?" The Djin grimaced. "Sahib, he sounds positively suicidal. Nobody in their right mind comes to Perv voluntarily . . . present company excepted, of course. Do you have any idea why he headed this way?"

I shrugged carelessly.

"It's not that hard to understand. He's a Pervect, so it's only natural that when things go wrong, he'd head for . . . "

"A Pervect?"

Kalvin was looking at me as if I'd just grown another head.

"You have one of these goons for a friend? And you admit it? And when he leaves you try to get him back?"

Now, I couldn't speak for any of the other citizens of Perv, but I knew Aahz was no goon. That's fact, not idle speculation. I knew the difference because I had two goons, Guido and Nunzio, working for me. I was about to point this out when it occurred to me that I wasn't required to give Kalvin any kind of explanation. I was the owner, and he was my servant.

"I rather think that's between my friend and me," I said stiffly. "As I understand it, your concern is to assist me in any way you can."

"Right-o," the Djin nodded, not seeming to take offense at my curtness. "Business it is. So what chore brings you to summon one of my ilk?"

"Simple enough. I'd like you to take me to my friend."

"Good for you. I'd like a pony and a red wagon, myself."

It was said so smoothly it took a moment for me to register what he had said.

"I beg your pardon?"

Kalvin shrugged.

"I said, 'I'd like a pony and . . .' "

"I know. I mean, I heard what you said," I interrupted. "I just don't understand. Are you saying you won't help me?"

"Not won't . . . can't. First of all, you've never even gotten around to telling me who your friend is."

"Oh, that's easy. His name is Aahz, and he's . . . "

" . . . And second of all, it's not within my powers. Sorry."

That stopped me. I had never paused to consider the extent of a Djin's power.

"It's not? But when I summoned you, I thought you were supposed to help me."

" . . . Any way I can," Kalvin finished. "Unfortunately for you, that doesn't cover a whole lot. How much did you pay for me, anyway?"

"A silver . . . but that was a while ago."

"A silver? Not bad. You must be pretty good at bargaining to get a Deveel to part with a registered Djin for that price."

I inclined my head at the compliment, but felt obliged to explain.

"He was in a state of shock at the time. The rest of his stock had been wiped out."

"Well, don't feel too proud," the Djin continued. "You

were still overcharged. I wouldn't pay a silver for my services.''

This was sounding less and less assuring. My easy solution to the problem seemed to be disappearing faster than a snowball on Deva.

''I don't get it,'' I said ''I always thought Djins were supposed to be heavy hitters in the magik department.''

Kalvin shook his head sadly.

''That's mostly sales hype,'' he admitted regretfully. ''Oh, some of the big boys can move mountains . . . literally. But those are top-of-the-line Djins and usually cost more than it would take to do the same things non-magikally. Small fry like me come cheaper, but we can't do whole bunches, either.''

''I'm sorry, Kalvin. None of this makes any sense. If Djins actually have less power than, say, your average magician for hire, why would anybody buy them at all?''

The Djin gestured grandly.

''The mystique . . . the status . . . do you know anything at all about Djinger?''

''Ginger? As in ginger beer?''

''No, Djin-ger . . . with a 'D' . . . As in the dimension where Djins and Djeanees come from.''

''I guess not.''

''Well, once upon a time, as the story goes, Djinger had a sudden disastrous drop in its money supply.''

This sounded a little familiar.

''An economic collapse? Like on Deva?''

The Djin shook his head.

''Embezzlement,'' he said. ''The entire Controller's office for the dimension disappeared, and when we finally found someone who could do an audit, it turned out most of the treasury was gone too.

"There was a great hue and cry, and several attempts to track the culprits, but the immediate problem was what to do for money. Manufacturing more wouldn't work, since it would simply devalue what we did have. What we really needed was a quick influx of funds from outside the dimension.

"That's when some marketing genius hit on the 'Djin In A Bottle' concept. Nearly everyone in the dimension who had the least skill or potential for magik was recruited for service. There was resistance, of course, but the promoters insisted it called for temporary contracts only, so the plan went into effect. In fact, the limited contract thing became a mainstay of the sales pitch . . . the mystique I was mentioning. That's why most Djins have conditions attached . . . three wishes only or whatever, though some are more ethical than others about how the wishes are fulfilled."

A thought suddenly occurred to me.

"Um, Kalvin? How many wishes do I get from you? Like I said, the Deveel was a bit shell-shocked and never said anything about limitations."

" . . . On wishes *or* powers, eh?" the Djin winked. "Not surprising. Shell-shocked or not, Deveels still know how to sell. In their own way they're truly amazing."

"How many?"

"What? Oh. I'm afraid my contract only calls for one wish, Skeeve. But don't worry, I'll play it clean. No tricks, no word traps. If you're only going to get one for your money, it's only fair that it's legit."

"I see," I said. "So what *can* you do?"

"Not much, actually. What I'm best at is bad jokes."

"Bad jokes?"

"You know, like 'How do you make a djin fizz?'"

"I don't think . . . "

"Drop him in acid. How do you . . . "

"I get the picture. That's it? You tell bad jokes?"

"Well, I give pretty good advice."

"That's good. I think I'm going to need some."

"I'll say. Well, the first piece of advice I've got for you is to forget about this and head for home before it's too late."

For a moment the thought was almost tempting, but I shook it off.

"Not a chance," I said firmly. "Let's go back to my original request. Can you advise me on how to find Aahz?"

"I might have a few ideas on the subject," the Djin admitted.

"Good."

"Have you tried a phone book?"

By now suspicion had grown into full-blown certainty. My hidden ace had turned out to be a deuce . . . no, a joker. If I was counting on Kalvin for the difference between success and failure, I was in a lot of trouble.

Until now I had taken finding Aahz for granted, and had only been worrying about what to say once we were face-to-face. Now, looking at the streets and skyscrapers of Perv, I was painfully aware that just *finding* Aahz was going to be harder than I thought . . . a *lot* harder!

Chapter Three:

"It's not even a nice place to visit!"
— FODOR'S *Guide To Perv*

EVEN AFTER GETTING used to the madness that was the Bazaar at Deva, the streets of Perv were something to behold. For one thing, the Bazaar was primarily geared for pedestrian traffic, the Merchants' Guild being strong enough to push through ordinances that favor modes and speed of travel that almost forced people to look at every shop and display they passed. My home dimension of Klah was a pretty backward place, and I had rarely seen a vehicle more advanced or faster than an oxcart.

Perv, on the other hand, had thoroughfares split between foot and vehicle traffic, and, for an unsophisticated guy like me, the vehicle traffic in particular was staggering. Literally hundreds of contraptions of as many descriptions jostled and snarled at each other at every intersection as they clawed for a better position in the seemingly senseless tangle of streets through which the torrent surged. Almost as incredible as the variety of vehicles was the collection of beasts which provided the locomotive power, pushing or pulling

their respective burdens while adding their voices to the
cacophony which threatened to drown out all other sounds
or conversation. Of course, they also added their contribu-
tion to the filth in the streets and smells in the air. It might
be the metropolitan home of millions of beings, but Perv
had the charm and aroma of a swamp.

What concerned me most at the moment, however, was
the traffic. Walking down the street on Perv was a little like
trying to swim upstream through a logjam. I was constantly
having to dodge and slide around citizens who seemed intent
on walking through the space I was already occupying. Not
that they seemed to be trying to hit me deliberately, mind
you. It's just that nobody except me seemed to be looking
where they were going. In fact, just making eye contact
was apparently a rare occurence.

"This friend of yours must really be something for you
to put up with this," Kalvin commented drily.

He was hovering in the vicinity of my shoulder, so I had
no difficulty hearing him over the din. I had worried about
how it would look having a Djin tagging along with me,
but it seems that while they're under control Djins can only
be seen and heard by their owner. It occurred to me that this
was fairly magikal and therefore in direct contrast to the
line Kalvin was selling me about how powerless he was.
He in turn assured me that it was really nothing, simply
part of a Djin's working tools that would be no help to me
at all. I wasn't assured. Somehow I had the feeling he wasn't
telling me everything about his abilities or lack thereof, but
having no way to force additional information out of him,
I magnanimously decided to let it ride.

"He's more than a friend," I said, not realizing I was
slipping into the explanation I had decided earlier not to
give. "He was my teacher, and then my business partner

as well. I probably owe him more than any other person in my life.''

'' . . . But not enough to respect his wishes,'' the Djin supplied carelessly.

That brought me to a dead stop, ignoring the crush and jostling of the other pedestrians.

''What's that supposed to mean?''

''Well, it's true, isn't it? This guy Aahz obviously wants to be left alone or he wouldn't have walked out on you, but you're determined to drag him back. To me that doesn't sound like you really care much about what's important to *him*.''

That hit uncomfortably close to home. As near as I could tell Aahz had left because I had been rather inconsiderate in my dealings with him. Still, I wasn't going to turn back now. At the very least I wanted a face-to-face talk before I let him disappear from my life.

''He was a bit upset and throwing a snit-fit at the time,'' I muttered, avoiding the question of my motives completely. ''I just want him to know that he's welcome if he wants to come back.''

With that I resumed my progress down the street. Half a dozen steps later, however, I realized the Djin was laughing ruefully.

''Now what?''

''Skeeve, you're really something, you know?'' Kalvin said, shaking his head. ''Perverts . . . excuse me, Pervects . . . are feared throughout the dimension for their terrible, violent tempers. But you, you not only describe it as a snit-fit, you're willing to show up on Perv itself just to make a point. You're either very good or an endangered species.''

It suddenly occurred to me that I wasn't making as much use of my Djin as I might. I mean, he *had* said that one of the things he was good at was advice, hadn't he?

"I don't know, Kalvin. I've never had much trouble with them. In fact, one of the things Aahz told me was that Pervects manufacture and spread a lot of the bad rumors about themselves just to discourage visitors."

"Oh, yeah?"

The Djin seemed unconvinced.

"Well, let's see then. Could you share some of the things you've heard about this dimension with me?"

Kalvin shrugged.

"If you want. I remember hearing about how one of your buddy's fellow citizens ripped off some guy's head and spit down his throat . . . literally!"

I ducked around a heavyset couple who were bearing down on me.

"Uh-huh. I heard the same rumor, but the one doing the ripping was a Troll, not a Pervect. Nobody actually *saw* that one, either. Besides, right now I'm more interested in information about the dimension than hearing tales of individual exploits."

I thought I lost Kalvin for a moment when I flattened against a wall to avoid a particularly muscular individual and the Djin didn't make the move with me, but when I stepped out again he was back in his now-accustomed place.

"Well, why didn't you say so, if that's what you wanted to hear?" he said as if there had been no interruption. "About Perv itself. Let me think. There's not that much information floating around, but what there is . . . Ah! Got it!"

He plucked a thick book out of thin air and started leafing through it. I was so eager to hear what he had to say that I didn't comment on that little stunt at the moment, but I also vowed anew to inquire further into Kalvin's "meager powers" when the opportunity presented itself.

"Let's see . . . Parts . . . P'boscus . . . Perv! You want

the statistics or should I skip to the good part?''

''Just give me the meat for now.''

''Okay. It says here, and I quote, 'Perv: One of the few dimensions where magik and technology have advanced equally through the ages. This blend has produced a culture and lifestyle virtually unique in the known dimensions. *Perverts* are noted for their arrogance, since they strongly believe that their dimension possesses the best of everything, and they are extremely vocal in that belief wherever they go. This is despite ample proof that other dimensions which have specialized in magik or technology exclusively have clearly surpassed Perv in both fields. Unfortunately, Pervects are also disproportionately strong and are *notorious for their bad tempers and ferocity,* so few care to argue the point with them.' End quote.''

Coming from Klah, a dimension which excelled at neither magik nor technology, I found the writeup to be pretty impressive. Kalvin, on the other hand, seemed to find endless amusement in it.

'' . . . 'Despite ample proof . . . ' I love it!'' he chortled. ''Wait'll the next time I see that blowhard.''

For some reason, I found this vaguely annoying.

''Say, Kalvin,'' I said, ''what does your book say about Djinger?''

''What book?''

''The one you . . . ''

I took my eyes off the foot traffic and glanced at him. He was dusting his hands innocently. The book was nowhere in sight.

I was opening my mouth to call him on his little disappearing act when something piled into me and sent me careening into a wall hard enough to make me see stars.

''Where do you think you're goin', Runt?''

This last came from the pudgy individual I had just col-

lided with. He had stopped to confront me and stood with
his fists clenched, leaning slightly forward as if being held
back by invisible companions. Fat or not, he looked tough
enough to walk through walls.

"Excuse me . . . I'm sorry," I mumbled, shaking my
head slightly to try to clear the spots that still danced in
front of my eyes.

"Well . . . watch it next time," he growled. He seemed
almost reluctant to break off our encounter, but finally spun
on his heel and marched on down the sidewalk.

"You shouldn't let that fat lug bluff you like that," Kalvin
advised. "Stand up to him."

"What makes you think he was bluffing?" I said, resum-
ing my journey, taking care to swerve around the other
Pervects crowding the path. "Besides, there's also the minor
detail that he was big enough to squash me like a bug."

"He raised a good point, though," the Djin continued
as if I hadn't spoken. "Just where *are* we going, anyway?"

"Down the street."

"I meant, 'what's our destination?' I thought you said
the phone book was no help."

Despite its millions of inhabitants, the Pervish phone book
we found had turned out to have less than a dozen pages.
Apparently unlisted phone numbers were *very* big in this
dimension, just one more indication of the social nature of
the citizens. Of course, leafing vainly through it, it had
occurred to me that Aahz had been with me off-dimension
for so long that it was doubtful he would have been in the
book even if it contained a full listing.

"I repeat, we're going down the street," I repeated.
"Beyond that, I don't know where we're going. Is that what
you wanted to hear?"

"Then why are we moving at all?" the Djin pressed.

"Wouldn't it be better to wait until we decided on a course of action before we started moving?"

I dodged around a slow-moving couple.

"I think better when I'm walking. Besides, I don't want to draw unnecessary attention to us by lurking suspiciously in alleys while I come up with a plan."

"Hey, you! Hold it a minute!"

This last was blasted with such volume that it momentarily dominated the street noise. Glancing behind me, I saw a uniformed Pervect who looked like a giant bulldog with scales bearing down on me with a purposeful stride.

"What's that?" I said, almost to myself.

Of course, unlike the direct questions I had put to him, Kalvin decided to answer this one.

"I believe it's what you referred to as 'unnecessary attention' . . . also known in some dimensions as a cop."

"I can see that. I just can't understand what he wants with me."

"What did you say?" the cop demanded, heaving to a halt in front of me.

"Me? Nothing," I replied, barely remembering in time that he couldn't see or hear Kalvin. "What's the trouble, officer?"

"Maybe you are. We'll see. What's your name?"

"Don't tell him!" Kalvin whispered in my ear.

"Why?" I said, the words slipping out before I had a chance to think.

"Because it's my job to keep track of suspicious characters," the cop growled, taking my question as being directed at him.

"Me? What have I done that's suspicious?"

"I've been following you for a couple of blocks now, and I've seen how you keep swervin' around folks. I even saw you apologize to someone and . . . say, I'll ask the questions here. Now, what's your name?"

"Tell him to bag it!" Kalvin advised. "He doesn't have a warrant or anything."

"Skeeve, sir," I supplied, desperately trying to ignore the Djin. All I needed now was to get in trouble with the local authorities. "Sorry if I'm acting strange, but I'm . . . not from around here and I'm a little disoriented."

I decided at the last moment to try to keep my off-dimension origins a secret. The policeman seemed to be fooled by my disguise spell, and I saw no point in enlightening him unless asked directly.

"You're being too polite!" the Djin whispered insistantly. "That's what made him suspicious in the first place, remember?"

"Not from around here, eh?" the cop snarled. "So tell me, Mr. Can't-Walk-Like-Normal-Folks-Skeeve, just where is it you're from . . . *exactly*?"

So much for keeping my origins a secret.

"Well, I was born on Klah, but lately I've been living at the Bazaar at Deva where I . . . "

"From off-dimension! I might have known. I suppose comin' from Deva that you're going to try to tell me you're here on business."

"Well, sort of. I'm here looking for my business partner."

"Another one from off-dimension! Any more and we'll have to fumigate the whole place."

The cop's mouth was starting to get on my nerves, but I thought it wise to keep a rein on my temper, despite the warning from Kalvin.

"Actually, he's from here. That is, he's a Pervect."

"A Pervect? Now I've heard everything. A fellow from off-dimension who claims to have a Pervect for a business partner!"

That did it.

"That's right!" I barked. "What's more, he happens to be my best friend. We had a fight and I'm trying to find him and get him to rejoin the company. What's it to you, anyway?"

The cop gave ground a little, then scowled at me.

"Well, I guess you're tellin' the truth. Even someone from off-dimension could come up with a better lie than that. Just watch your step, fella. We don't like outsiders much on Perv."

He gave me one last hard glare, then wandered off, glancing back at me from time to time. Still a little hot under the collar, I matched him glare for glare.

"That's better," Kalvin chortled, reminding me of his presence. "A Klahd, huh? That explains a few things."

"Oh, yeah? Like what?"

Like I said, I was still a little miffed.

"Like why we've been wandering around without a plan. You aren't used to metropolises this size, are you?"

Mad as I was, I couldn't argue with that.

"Well . . . "

"If you don't mind, could I offer you a little advice without your asking for it?"

I shrugged non-committally.

"It's obvious to me this little search of yours could take some time. It might be a good idea if we hunted up a hotel to use for a base camp. If that cop had asked where you were staying on Perv, things might have gotten a little awkward."

That made sense. It also brought home to me just how much of a stranger in a strange land I was. On most of my adventures I had either slept under the stars or had housing provided by friends or business associates. Consequently, I had remarkably little experience with hotels . . . like none.

"Thanks, Kalvin," I said, regaining a bit of my normal composure. "So how do you recommend we find a hotel?"

"We could hail a cab and ask the driver."

Terrific. The Djin was being his normal, helpful self. I was beginning to feel some things weren't going to change.

Chapter Four:

"Taxis are water soluble."

—G. KELLY

"I'LL TELL YA, this would be a pretty nice place, if it weren't for all the Perverts."

The taxi driver said this the same way he had made all his comments since picking us up: over his shoulder while carelessly steering his vehicle full tilt through the melee of traffic.

I had ignored most of his chatter, which didn't seem to bother him. He apparently didn't expect a response, but this last comment caught my interest.

"Excuse me, but aren't you a Pervert . . . I mean, a Pervect?"

The driver nodded vigorously and half turned in his seat to face me.

"There. See what I mean?"

Frankly, I didn't. If there was logic in his statement, it escaped my comprehension. What I did see, however, was that we were still plunging forward without slacking our speed. There was a tangle of stopped vehicles ahead which

31

the driver seemed oblivious to as he tried to make his con-
versational point. A collision seemed inescapable.

"Look out!" I shouted, pointing frantically at the obstruc-
tions.

Without losing eye contact, the driver's hand lashed out
and smashed down on the toy stuffed goose that was taped
down in front of him. The thing let out a harsh, tremendous
"HONK!!" that would have gotten it named king of the
geese if they ever held an election.

"Anyway, that's what I'm talkin' about." The driver
finished and turned his attention forward again.

The traffic jam had miraculously melted away before he
had finished speaking, and we sailed through the intersection
unscathed.

"Relax, Skeeve," Kalvin laughed. "This guy's a professional."

"A professional what?" I muttered.

"How's that?" the driver said, starting to turn again.

"NOTHING! I . . . nothing."

I had been unimpressed with the taxi since it had picked
us up. Actually, 'picked us up' is much too mild a phrase
and doesn't begin to convey what had actually happened.

Following Kalvin's instructions, I had stepped to the curb
and raised my hand.

"Like this?" I said, making the mistake of turning my
head to ask him directly.

Facing away from the street, I missed what happened
next, which is probably just as well. The normal traffic din
suddenly erupted with shrieks and crashes. Startled, I jerked
my hand back and jumped sideways to a spot a safer distance
from the street. By the time I focused on the scene, most
of the noise and the action had ceased.

Traffic was backed up behind the vehicle crouched at the
curb beside us, and blocked drivers were leaning out to

shout and/or shake their fists threateningly. There may have been a few collisions, but the condition of most of the vehicles on the street was such that I couldn't be certain which damages were new and which were scars from earlier skirmishes.

"That's right," Kalvin said, apparently unruffled by the mayhem which had just transpired. "Get in."

"You're kidding!"

The vehicle which had stopped for us was not one to inspire confidence. It was sort of a box-like contraption hanging between two low-slung, tailless lizards. The reptiles had blindfolds wrapped around their head obscuring their eyes, but they kept casting from side to side while their tongues lashed in and out questing for data on their surroundings. Simply put, they looked powerful and hungry enough for me to want to keep my distance.

"Maybe we should wait for another one," I suggested hopefully.

"Get in," the Djin ordered. "If we block traffic too long the cop will be back."

That was sufficient incentive for me, and I bravely entered the box and took a seat behind the driver, Kalvin never leaving my shoulder. The interior of the box seemed safe enough. There were two seats in the rear where I was sitting, and another beside the driver, although the latter seemed filled to overflowing with papers and boxes that would occasionally spill to the floor when we took a corner too fast . . . which was always. There were notes and pictures pinned and taped to the walls and ceiling in a halo around the driver, and a confusing array of dials and switches on the panel in front of him. Basically, one had the suspicion the driver lived in his vehicle, which was vaguely reassuring. I mean, the man wouldn't do anything to endanger his own home, would he?

"Where to?" the driver said, casually forcing his vehicle back into the flow of traffic.

"Um, just take me to a hotel."

"Expensive . . . cheap . . . what?"

"Oh, something moderate, maybe a bit on the inexpensive side."

"Right."

I was actually pretty well set financially. A money belt around my waist had over two thousand in gold I had brought along to cover expenses on my search. Still, there was no sense throwing it away needlessly, and I figured since I didn't plan to spend much time in my room, I wouldn't need anything particularly grand.

Within the first few blocks, however, I had pause to reconsider the wisdom of my choice of vehicles. As far as I could tell, the lizards were blindfolded to prevent their animal survival instinct from interfering with the driver's orders. I couldn't figure out how he was controlling them, but he seemed determined to maintain a breakneck pace regardless of minor considerations like safety and common sense.

"So, have you two been on Perv long?"

The driver's voice dragged me back to the present my mind had been trying so desperately to ignore.

"Just got here today. In fact."

Suddenly, I zeroed in on what he had said.

"Excuse me, did you say 'you *two*'?"

The driver bobbed his head in acknowledgment.

"That's right. It isn't often I get a Klahd or a Djin, much less one of each in the same fare."

He not only knew how many we were, he had spotted *what* we were! Needless to say, the news was not welcome.

"What the . . . " Kalvin started, but I silenced him with a gesture.

"Before I answer, do you mind my asking how you knew?" I said, casually glancing around to see if there was a way we could exit rapidly if necessary.

"Scanned you when you got in," the driver said, pointing briefly to a small screen amidst the clutter of his other devices. "A cabbie can't be too careful these days . . . not with the crime rate the way it is. We're moving targets for every amateur stick-up artist or hijacker who needs a quick bankroll. I had that baby installed so I'd know in advance what was sittin' down behind me."

He shot me a quick wink over his shoulder.

"Don't worry, though. I won't charge you extra for the Djin. He don't take up much space. So far as I can tell, you two are harmless enough."

That reassured me, at least to a point where I no longer considered jumping from the moving vehicle.

"I take it you don't share the general low opinion of folks from off-dimension?"

"Don't make no never mind to me, as long as you pay your way," the driver waved. "As far as I can tell, you got enough money on ya that I don't think you'll try to welch on anything as piddling as a cab fare. Keep up the disguise, though. Some of the merchants around here will raise their prices at the sight of someone from off-dimension just to make you feel unwelcome . . . and things are already priced sky-high."

"Thanks for the warning."

" . . . And you might be careful carrying so much cash. Everything you've heard about crime on the streets in this place is true. In fact, you'd probably be best off hiring yourself a bodyguard while you're here. If you want, I can recommend a couple good ones."

"You know, that might not be a bad idea," Kalvin said. "In case I hadn't mentioned it, Djinger is a pretty peaceful dimension. I won't be much help to you in a fight.''

I ignored him as the cabbie continued, apparently unable to hear the Djin despite his various devices. Remembering some of the dangers I had faced in my adventures, the idea of hiring someone to guard me just to walk down the street seemed a little ludicrous.

''I appreciate your concern, but I'm pretty good at looking out for myself.''

''Suit yourself, it was just a suggestion. Say, you want something to eat? I sell snack packs.''

He used one hand to pick up a box from the seat beside him and shove it in my direction. It was filled with small bags with stuff oozing through the sides.

''Uh . . . not just now, thanks,'' I said, trying to fight down the sudden queasiness I felt.

The driver was not to be daunted. He tossed the box back onto the seat and snatched up a booklet.

''How about a guidebook, then? I write and print 'em myself. It's better'n anything you'll find on the stands . . . and cheaper, too.''

That might have come in handy, but glancing at it I could see the print was a series of squiggles and hieroglyphics that were meaningless to me. I always travel with a translator pendant to get around the language barrier, but unfortunately its powers don't extend to the written word.

''I don't suppose you have a Klahdish translation, do you?''

''Sorry,'' he said, tossing the booklet in the same general direction the box had gone. ''I'm takin' a few courses to try to learn some other languages, but Klahdish isn't one of them. Not enough demand, ya know?''

Despite my continuing concern over his attention to his driving, the cabbie was beginning to interest me.

''I must say you're enterprising enough. Cab driver, publisher, cook, translator . . . is there anything else you do?''

"Oh, I'm into a lot of things. Photography, tour guide . . .
I even draw a little. Some of these drawings I did. I'd be
willing to part with them for the right price."

He gestured at some of the sheets adorning the interior,
and the cab veered dangerously to the right.

"Ah . . . actually, I was interested in something else you
said just now."

"Yeah? What's that?"

"Tour guide."

"Oh, that. Sure. I love to when I get the chance. It's
sweet money. Beats the heck out of fighting the other hacks
for fares all day long."

I glanced at Kalvin and raised a questioning eyebrow.

"Go ahead," he said. "We could use a guide, and you
seem to be getting along with this guy pretty well. You
know what they say, 'Better the Deveel you know.' ''

Obviously the Djin's knowledge did not extend to Deveels, but this wasn't the time or place to instruct him. I
turned my attention back to the driver.

"I was thinking of hiring you more as a guide than a tour
guide. How much do you make a day with this cab?''

"Well, on a good day I can turn better than a hundred."

"Uh-huh," I said. "How about on an average day?"

That earned me another over-the-shoulder glance.

"I gotta say, fella, you sure don't talk like a Klahd."

"I live at the Bazaar at Deva," I smiled. "It does wonders
for your bargaining skills. How much?"

We haggled back and forth for a few minutes, but even-
tually settled on a figure. It seemed fair, and I wasn't exactly
in a position to be choosy. If the device the cabbie had used
was widespread in his profession, my disguise would be
blown the second I stepped into a cab, and there was no
guarantee the next driver would be as well disposed toward

off-dimensioners as our current junior entrepreneur.

"Okay, you've got yourself a guide," the driver said at last. "Now, who am I working for?"

"I'm Skeeve, and the Djin with me is Kalvin."

"Don't know about the Djin," the cabbie shrugged. "Either he don't talk much or I can't hear him. Pleased to meetcha, though, Mr. Skeeve. I'm Edvik."

He extended a hand into the back seat, which I shook cautiously. I had encountered Pervish handshakes before and could still feel them in my joints in wet weather.

"So, where do you want to go first?"

That seemed like a strange question to me, but I answered it anyway.

"To a hotel, same as before."

"Uh-uh."

"Excuse me?" I said, puzzled.

"Hey, you hired a guide, you're going to get one. You're about to check into a hotel, right?"

"That's right."

"Well, you try to check into a Pervish hotel the way you are, without luggage, and they're going to give you a rough time whether they figure you're from off-dimension or not. They'll be afraid that you're trying to get access to a room to steal the furniture or maybe to try to break into other rooms on the same floor."

That was a new concept to me. While I had a fairly extensive wardrobe at home, I usually traveled light when I was working . . . like with the clothes I was wearing and money. It had never occurred to me that a lack of luggage would cause people to be suspicious of my intentions.

"What do you think, Kalvin?"

"Beats me," the Djin shrugged "I've never run into the problem. Of course, I travel in a bottle and people can't see me anyway."

"Well, what do you recommend, Edvik?"

"Let me take you by a department store. You can pick up a small bag there and maybe some stuff to put in it. Believe me, it'll pay in the long run in dealing with a hotel."

I pondered the point for a moment, then decided it was senseless to hire a guide, then not listen to his advice.

"All right," I said at last. "How far is it to this store you were talking about?"

"Oh, not far at all. Hang on!"

This last warning was a bit late, as he had already thrown the cab into a tight U-turn which scrambled the traffic around us and sent me tumbling across the seat. Before I could recover my balance we were well on our way back in the direction we had come from.

As accustomed as I was to madcap excursions, it occurred to me that this one was quickly becoming more complex than anything I had previously experienced. I hoped the education would prove to be more enjoyable and beneficial than it had been so far.

Chapter Five:

"I just need to pick up a few things."
—I. MARCOS

I'VE MADE NUMEROUS references to the Bazaar at Deva, where I make my home. For the benefit of those who do not travel the dimensions or read these books, it's the largest market center in the known dimensions. Anything you can imagine, as well as many an item you can't, is for sale there. Competition is stiff, and the Deveel merchants will turn themselves or their customers inside out before they'll let a sale get away.

I mention this so that everyone following this adventure will realize what a shock shopping on Perv was to me. The differences were so many, it was almost hard to accept that the same activity was underway in both instances.

For openers, there was the basic layout. The Bazaar is an endless series of stalls and shops that stretch over the horizon in all directions. There are various concentrations of specialty shops, to be sure, but no real pattern and, more important, no way of finding anything without looking. In direct contrast, Pervish shopping is dominated by what Edvik referred to as "department stores." One store could take up an entire city block with as many as six stories crammed full of merchandise. The goods are organized into sections or "departments" and carefully controlled so as not to be in competition with each other. Signs are prominently displayed to tell shoppers where everything is, though it is still relatively easy to get lost in the maze of aisles and counters. Of course, it also helps if you can read Pervish.

Perhaps the biggest difference, however is in the general attitude toward customers. This was apparent when I made my first stop in the luggage department.

There was a good selection of bags and cases there, and the displays were laid out well enough so that I could distinguish between the magikal and non-magikal bags without being able to read the signs. It wasn't even that hard to make my selection. There was a small canvas suitcase roughly the size of a thick attache case which caught my eye both from the simplicity of the design and the fact that it was magikally endowed. That is, it had a permanent spell on it which made it about three times as large on the inside as it showed on the exterior. It occurred to me it might be a handy item to have, and if I was going to buy something to check into a hotel with, it might as well be something I could actually get some use out of later. The difficulties started when I was ready to make my purchase.

Up to this point, I had been pleasantly surprised that the sales help had left me alone. On Deva, I would have been approached by the proprietor or one of his assistants as soon as I set foot in the display area, and it was kind of nice for a change to browse leisurely without being pressured or having whatever overstock was on sale that day touted to the heavens. Once I had made my selection, however, I found that getting the attention of one of the salesmen was astoundingly difficult.

Standing by the display which featured the bag I wanted, I looked toward the cash register where two salesmen were engrossed in conversation. On Deva, this would have been all that was necessary to have the proprietor swoop down on me, assuming he had given me any room to start with. Here, they didn't seem to notice. Slightly puzzled, I waited a few moments, then cleared my throat noisily. It didn't even earn me a glance.

"Are you coming down with something, Skeeve?" Kalvin said anxiously. "Anything contagious, I mean?"

"No, I'm just trying to signal for one of the salesmen."

"Oh."

The Djin floated a few feet higher to peer toward the cash register.

"It doesn't seem to be working."

"I can see that, Kalvin. The question is, what will?"

We waited a few more moments and watched the salesmen in their discussion.

"Maybe you should go over there," the Djin suggested at last.

It seemed strange to pursue a salesman to get him to take my money, but lacking a better idea I wandered over to the sales counter.

. . . And stood there.

The salesmen finished their discussion of sports and started on dirty jokes.

. . . And stood there.

Then the subject was the relative merits of the women they were dating. It might have been interesting, not to mention instructional, if I hadn't been getting so annoyed.

"Do you get the feeling I'm not the only one who's invisible?" Kalvin muttered sarcastically.

When a Djin who's used to sitting in a bottle for years starts getting impatient, I figure I'm justified in taking action.

"Excuse me," I said firmly, breaking into the conversation. "I'd like to look at that bag over there? The small magik one in green canvas?"

"Go ahead," one of the salesmen shrugged and returned to his conversation.

I stood there for a few more moments in sheer disbelief, then turned and marched back over to the bag.

"Now you're starting to move like a Pervect," the Djin observed.

"I don't care," I snarled. "And that's *Pervert!* I've tried to be nice . . . didn't want to mess up their display . . . *but*, if they insist . . ."

For the next several minutes I took my anger out on the bag, which was probably the safest object to vent my spleen on. I hefted it, swung it over my head, slammed it against the floor a couple times, and did everything else to it I could think of short of climbing inside. I've got to admit the thing was sturdily made. Then again, I was starting to see why goods on Perv had to be tough. The salesmen never favored me with so much as a glance.

"Check me on this, Kalvin," I panted, my exertions finally starting to wear on my endurance. "The price tag on this bag *does* say 125 gold, doesn't it?"

I may not be able to read many written languages, but numbers and prices have never given me any trouble. I guess it comes from hanging around with Aahz as long as I have . . . not to mention Tananda and Bunny.

"That's the way I read it."

"I mean, that's not exactly cheap. I've seen clerks treat 10-copper items with more concern and respect than these guys are showing. Don't they care?"

"Not so's you'd notice," the Djin agreed.

"Do you think they'd notice if I tried to just tuck it under my arm and walk out without paying? It would be nice to know *something* can get to these guys.''

The Djin glanced around nervously.

''I really don't know, but I don't think you should try.''

That cooled me down a bit. I was still in strange territory on a mission, and it was no time to start testing security systems.

''Okay,'' I growled. ''Let's try this again.''

This time, when I approached the sales counter, I figured I had learned my lesson. No more Mr. Nice Guy. No more waiting around for them to end their discussion.

''I'd like to buy that green magik bag, the small canvas one,'' I said, bursting into their conversation in mid-sentence.

''All right.''

The salesman I had first spoken with was halfway to the display before I realized what he was doing. Now that I had his attention, my normal shopping instincts cut in.

''Excuse me. I'd like a new case rather than the floor display . . . and is there any chance you have it in black?''

The salesman gave me a long martyred look.

''Just a moment, I'll have to check.''

He went slouching off while his partner began wandering aimlessly through the section straightening displays.

''If you don't mind my saying so, Skeeve, I think you're pushing your luck,'' Kalvin observed.

''Hey, it's worth asking,'' I shrugged. ''Besides, however inconsiderate the help is, this is still a store. There's got to be some interest in giving the customer what he wants.''

Fifteen minutes later, the salesman still hadn't reappeared and I found my temper was starting to simmer again.

''Um . . . is it time to say 'I told you so' yet?'' the Djin smirked.

Ignoring him, I intercepted the second salesman.

''Excuse me, how far is it to the storeroom?''

"Why do you ask?" he blinked.

"Well, your partner was checking on something for me, and it's been a while."

The salesman grimaced.

"Who? Him? He's gone on break. He should be back in an hour or so if you'd like to wait."

"What??"

"I suppose I could go look for you, if you'd like. What was it you wanted?"

As I've said before, I may be slow, but I *do* learn. This was the last salesman in the section and I wasn't about to let him out of my sight.

"Forget it. I'll take the small green magik bag over there. The one in canvas."

"Okay. That'll be 125 in gold. Do you want to carry it or shall I give you a sack?"

Before I could think, my Bazaar reflexes cut in.

"Just a second. That's 125 for a new bag. How much will you knock off the price for one that's been used for a floor display?"

Kalvin groaned and covered his eyes with one hand.

"I don't set the prices," the salesman said, starting to turn away. "If you don't like it, shop somewhere else."

The thought of starting this fiasco all over again defeated me.

"Wait a minute," I called, fumbling with my money belt. "I'll take it. But can I at least get a receipt?"

Shopping for clothes turned out to be a trial of a different sort. There were magik lifts that carried me up two floors to the clothing section, which fortunately gave me time to think things through.

The trouble was that I was disguised as a Pervect. Because of their build, this made me appear much more heavyset

than I really was. If I bought clothes to fit my disguised
form, they'd hang on the real me like a tent. If I went for
my real size, however, it would be a dead giveaway when
I asked to try them on.

What I finally decided to do was to shop in the kids'
section, which would be the best bet for finding my real
size anyway, and say I was buying them for my son. I had
gotten pretty good at eyeballing clothes for size, so the fit
probably wouldn't be too bad.

I needn't have worried.

It seems a lot more people shop for clothes than shop for
luggage. A *lot* more.

Not being able to read the signs, I couldn't tell if there
was a sale on or if this was the normal volume of customers
the section got. Whatever the case, the place was a
madhouse. Throngs of shoppers, male and female, jostled
and clawed at each other over tables heaped with various
items of apparel. To say angry voices were raised fails to
capture the shrieks and curses which assaulted my ears as
I approached the area, but I could make out the occasional
sounds of cloth tearing. Whether this was from items on
sale being ripped asunder by rival shoppers, or the rival
shoppers themselves being ripped asunder I could never tell
for sure. It was like watching a pileup at the Big Game,
but without teams and without breaks between plays.

"Don't tell me you're going into that!" Kalvin gasped.
"Without armor or artillery?"

It seemed a strange question for someone from a sup-
posedly peaceful dimension to ask, but I was busy concen-
trating on the task ahead.

"This shopping thing is already taking too long," I said
grimly. "I'm *not* going to lose any more time by having
Edvik hunt us up another store . . . especially since there's

no guarantee it will be any better than this one. I'm going
to wade in there, grab a couple of outfits, and be done with
it once and for all.''

Good taste and a queasy stomach at the memory prevent
me from going into detail on how the next half hour went.
Suffice it to say that Kalvin abandoned me and hovered
near the ceiling to watch and wait until I was done. Now
I've knocked around a bit, and *been* knocked around more
times than I care to recall, but if there's any memory that
compares to holding my own against a mob of Pervish
shoppers, my mind has successfully suppressed it. I elbowed
and shoved, used more than a little magik when no one was
looking and called on most of the dirty tricks I learned in
the Big Game, and in the end I had two outfits I wasn't
wild about but was willing to settle for rather than enter the
fracas anew in search of something better. I also had a
lingering fondness for the fat Pervish lady I hid behind from
time to time to catch my breath.

Having sat out the battle, Kalvin was in good shape to
guide me back to the exit. That was fortunate, since the
adrenalin drop after emerging from the brawl was such that
I could barely see straight, let alone walk steadily.

I don't know where Edvik was waiting, but his cab
materialized out of the traffic as soon as we emerged from
the store and in no time we were back in the safety of the
back seat. It wasn't until later that I realized what a commen-
tary it was on department stores that the cab now seemed
safe to me.

"Can we go to the hotel now?" I said, sinking back in
the seat and shutting my eyes.

"Like that? Don't you want to change first?"

"Change?" Somehow I didn't like the sound of that.

"You know, into a conservative suit. Business types always get the best service at hotels."

Kalvin groaned, but he needn't have worried. If there was one thing I knew for sure, it's that I wasn't heading back to that store.

"Tell you what, Edvik. Describe a suit to me."

The cabbie rubbed his chin as he plotted his way through the traffic.

"Well, let's see. They're usually dark grey or black . . . three piece with a vest . . . thin white pinstripes closely spaced . . . and, you know, the usual accessories like a white shirt and a striped tie."

Just as I thought. The same as was worn on Deva . . . and every other dimension I've met businessmen on. I closed my eyes again and made a few adjustments to my disguise spell.

"Like this?"

The cabbie glanced over his shoulder, then swiveled around to gape openly.

"Say! That's neat!" he exclaimed.

"Thank you," I said smugly. "It's nothing really. Just a disguise spell I use."

"So why didn't you use that to fake the new outfits and the luggage instead of hassling with the stores?"

"I was about to ask the same thing," Kalvin murmured.

For the life of me, I couldn't think of a good answer.

Chapter Six:

"There's no place like home!"

—Ḥ. JOHNSON

ONCE WE FINALLY arrived at the hotel Edvik had chosen to recommend, I was a bit put off by the sight. It had a sign that declared it to be The New Inn, but it looked like most of the other buildings we had seen so far, which is to say it was old, dilapidated, and covered with soot. Then again, even if its appearance had been better, the neighborhood it was in would have given me pause. Between the garbage in the streets and the metal shutters on the store windows, it wasn't an area in which I would normally be inclined to get out of the cab, much less rent a room. I was about to comment on this to my driver/guide, when I noticed the uniformed doorman and decided to make my inquiry a bit more gentle.

"Ah . . . this is the low-price hotel you've been figuring on?"

"It's about as low as you can go without ending up in a real dive," the cabbie shrugged. "Actually, it's a little nicer than most in the same price range. They've had to lower their prices because of the trouble they've been having.''

''Trouble?''

''Yeah. There's an ax murderer loose around here that the police haven't been able to catch. He's been killing about one a week . . . last week he got one right in the lobby.''

''Ax murderer??!''

''That's right. You don't have to worry about it, though.''

''How do you figure that?''

''Well, it's been going on for a month now, and since you're just checking in, and you've never been here before, there's not much chance they'll try to blame you for it.''

Actually, *that* hadn't been my worry. I had been more concerned with my odds on being the next victim. Before I could clarify this to Edvik, however, the doorman had jerked open the door of the cab and snatched up my bag.

''You'd better follow your bag and keep an eye on it,'' the driver advised. ''I'll be by in the morning to pick you up. Oh, and be sure to tip the baggage handler. Otherwise it may not be recognizable by the time you get it back.''

The lizards were already starting to move as he imparted this last piece of wisdom, so I dove for the door before the vehicle gathered too much momentum and I ended up permanently separated from my luggage. Needless or not, I had gone through far too much to get it to lose it now. Before I had pause to think that I was losing touch with my guide and advisor for this dimension, the cab had turned a corner and disappeared.

''I think this guy wants a tip,'' Kalvin said, gesturing toward the doorman. At least I still had the Djin with me.

I had to acknowledge his point. The uniformed Pervect was standing stuffily, with his palm up and a vague sneer on his face that would probably pass for a smile locally. I only hesitated a second before slipping him some loose change. Normally, I would expect someone to wait until *after* he had performed a service before hinting for a tip, but obviously things differed from dimension to dimension. This was probably what Edvik had been warning me about . . . that the doorman would want money *before* moving my bag, and that if the juice wasn't big enough, it was "Goodbye luggage!" In a way, it made sense.

My speculation on this philosophy was cut short when I noticed another person, a bellhop this time, picking up my bag and heading inside with it, leaving the doorman outside weighing the tip I had just given him in his hand. I began to smell a rat.

"Where is he going?" I said to the smug doorman, as casually as I could manage.

"To the front desk, sir."

"But he has my bag."

"Yes. I suggest you follow him closely. He's not to be trusted, you know."

"But . . . Ohhh . . . !"

I knew when I had been outmaneuvered. Apparently, all the doorman did was open cab doors and off-load the baggage . . . *not* carry the bags inside. Of course, the fact that I had tipped him assuming he would perform that service was my fault, not his. Defeated, I trailed after the bellhop, who was waiting inside with his hand out in the now all-too-familiar gesture that means "Pay or you'll never see the end of me." This time, however, I was more than happy to pay him off. Whatever Edvik had said, I had decided I would be better off handling my own luggage from here on out.

Kalvin muttered something in my ear about not paying the help until they had finished their work, but the bellhop seemed to understand what it was all about, since he disappeared as soon as I paid him. Ignoring Kalvin's grumbles,

I turned my attention to the hotel interior.

The reception area wasn't much larger than the space we used for similar purposes back at M.Y.T.H. Inc., except the furnishings were dominated by a huge counter which I assumed was what the doorman had referred to as the front desk. Of course, to my mind this made the lobby rather small since, as a hotel, this place was supposed to get more public traffic than our consulting offices did. Personally, I felt it boded ill for the size of the rooms. Then again, I had told Edvik to take us somewhere inexpensive. I supposed I couldn't expect low rates *and* stylish accomodations, and given a choice . . .

"May I help you?"

This last came from the Pervect behind the front desk. It might read polite, but the tone of his voice was that of one addressing someone who just walked through the front door with a box of garbage.

"Yes," I said, deciding to give pleasant one last try. "I'd like a room, please. A single."

The desk clerk looked as if I had just spat on the floor.

"Do you have reservations?"

The question surprised me a little, but I decided to stick with honesty.

"Well, I'm not wild about the neighborhood . . . and then there's the rumor about the ax murderer . . ."

"Skeeve . . . SKEEVE!!" Kalvin hissed desperately. "He means, 'Do you have a reservation for a room?'"

So much for honesty. I shot a look at the desk clerk, who was staring at me as if I had asked him to sell his first-born into slavery.

" . . . But, um, if you're asking if I reserved a room in advance, the answer is no," I finished lamely.

The clerk stared at me for a few more moments, then ran a practiced finger down a list on the desk in front of him.

"I'm afraid that all we have available at this time is one of our Economy Rooms. You really should reserve in advance for the best selection."

"An Economy Room will be fine," I assured him. "I'll need it for about a week."

"Very well," the clerk nodded, pushing a form at me across the desk, "If you'll just fill this out, the rate will be a hundred in gold."

I was glad I had been warned about prices on Perv. A hundred in gold seemed a bit steep to me, but having been forewarned I managed to hide my surprise as I reached for the form.

" . . . A day. Payable in advance, of course."

My hand stopped just short of the form.

"A hundred in gold a day?" I said as carefully as I could.

"Skeeve!" Kalvin yipped in my ear. "Remember, you were warned things were expensive here! This is a low-priced hotel, remember?"

"Payable in advance," the clerk confirmed.

I withdrew my hands from the desk.

"How much time do you want to spend looking for a room, Skeeve?" the Djin continued desperately. "The cab won't be back until morning and it's getting dark out. Do you really want to walk these streets at night?"

I took a hundred in gold from my money belt and dropped it on the desk, then started filling out the form.

"I assumed that *each day* is payable in advance, considering the interest rates," I said calmly. "Oh, yes, I'd like a receipt for that, as well."

The desk clerk whisked the form from under my pen and glanced at it almost before I had finished signing it.

"Quite right, Mr. . . Skeeve. I'll have a receipt for you in a moment."

It was nice to know some Pervects were efficient, once

56 Robert Asprin

you had met their price. The hundred in gold had already disappeared.

The desk clerk slipped the receipt across the desk, a key held daintily in his other hand. I claimed the receipt and was starting to go for the key when he casually moved it back out of my reach, slapping his palm down on a small bell that was on the desk.

"Front!"

Before I could ask what this little declaration was supposed to mean, a bellhop had materialized at my side . . . a different one than before.

"Room 242," the desk clerk declared, handing the bellhop my key.

"Yessir. Is this your luggage?"

"Well, yes. It's . . ."

Without waiting for me to finish, the bellhop snatched up my bag and started for the stairs, beckoning me to follow. I trailed along in his wake. At this point, I had had it with Pervects and hotels and tips. If this clown thought I was . . .

"Going to tip him?" Kalvin asked, floating around to hang in the air in front of me. Fortunately, he was translucent enough for me to see through him.

I gave him my toothiest smile.

"If that means 'No' like I think it does, you'd better reconsider."

Whether I needed to hear this or not, I definitely didn't want to. I deliberately let my gaze wander to the ceiling and promptly tripped over a step.

"Remember what Edvik said," the Djin continued insistently. "You need all the allies you can get. You can't afford to get vindictive with this guy."

Slowly, my irritation began to give way to common sense. Kalvin was right. If nothing else, I had heard that bellhops were prime sources of local information, and if being nice to this character would speed my search for Aahz, thereby shortening my stay on Perv, then it would definitely be worth at least a decent tip. Taking a deep breath, I caught the Djin's eye and gave a curt nod, whereupon he subsided. It occurred to me it was nice to deal with someone who would let an argument drop once he'd won it.

The bellhop unlocked a door and ushered me into my room with a flourish. The first view of my temporary headquarters almost reversed my mind all over again.

The room was what could only be politely referred to as a hole . . . and I wasn't in a particularly polite mood. For openers, it was small . . . smaller than most of the closets in my place back at the Bazaar. There was barely enough space to walk around the bed without scooting sideways, and what little room there was was cramped further by a small bureau which was missing the knob on one of the two drawers, and a chair which looked about as comfortable as a bed of nails. The shade of the bedside lamp was askew, and the wallpaper was torn with one large flap hanging loose except where it was secured by cobwebs. I couldn't tell if the texture of the carpet was dust or mildew, though from the smell I suspected the latter. The ceiling had large water-stains on it, but you couldn't tell without looking hard because the light in the place was dim enough to make a vampire feel claustrophobic. All this for a mere hundred in gold a night.

"Great view, isn't it?" the bellhop said, pulling the shades aside to reveal a window that hadn't been washed since the discovery of fire. At first I thought the curtain rod was sagging, but closer examination showed it had actually been nailed in place crooked.

"This is what you call a great view?"

That comment kind of slipped out despite my resolve. I had just figured out that it wasn't that the window was so dirty I couldn't see out of it. Rather, the view consisted of a blank stone wall maybe an arm's length away.

The bellhop didn't seem the least put out by my rhetorical question.

"You should see the view from the first floor," he shrugged. "All the rooms there look out onto the courtyard, which includes the garbage dump. At least this view doesn't have maggots."

My stomach tilted to the left and sank. Swallowing hard, I resolved not to ask any more questions about the room.

"Could you lay off about the view?" Kalvin whined desperately.

"Way ahead of you," I replied.

"How's that again?" the bellhop said, turning to face me.

"I said, 'I'll settle for this view,' " I amended hastily.

"Thought you would. No, sir, you don't see many rooms this good at these prices."

I realized he was looking at me expectantly for confirmation.

"I . . . I've never seen anything like it."

He kept looking at me. I cast about in my mind for something vaguely complimentary to say about the room.

"The tip, Skeeve! He's waiting for a tip!"

"Oh! Yes, of course."

I fumbled a few more coins out of my money belt.

"Thank you, sir," the bellhop nodded, accepting my offering. "And if you have any more questions, the name's Burgt."

He was heading for the door when it occurred to me I might make further use of his knowledge.

"Say . . . um, Burgt."

"Yes, sir?"

"Is there someplace around here I can get a bite to eat? Maybe someplace that specializes in off-dimension food?"

"Sure. There's a little place about half a block to your left as you come out of the main entrance. It's called Bandi's. You can't miss it."

That was worth a few extra coins to me. It also gave me an idea.

"Say, Burgt, I've heard you bellhops have a bit of an information network. Is that true?"

The bellhop eyed the coins I was pouring back and forth from hand to hand.

"Sort of," he admitted. "It depends on what kind of information you're looking for."

"Well, I'm looking for a guy, name of Aahz. Would have hit town in the last couple of days. If you or any of your friends should find out where he is and let me know, I'd be *real* appreciative. Get me?"

I let the coins pour into his uniform pocket.

"Yes, *sir*. Aahz, was it? I'll spread the word and see what we can turn up."

He departed hastily, shutting the door firmly but quietly behind him.

"You did that very well, Skeeve," Kalvin said.

"What? Oh. Thanks, Kalvin."

"Really. You looked just like a gangster paying off an informant."

I guess my work with the Mob had influenced me more than I had realized. It wasn't a line of conversation I wanted to pursue too far, though.

"Just something I picked up," I said casually, pocketing the room key. "Come on. Let's try to find something eatable in this dimension."

Chapter Seven:

"... On the street where you live."
—QUOTE FROM AN ANONYMOUS EXTORTION NOTE

I HAD THOUGHT the streets of Perv were intimidating walking or riding through them by day. At night, they were a whole new world. I didn't know if I shoud be frightened or depressed, but one thing I knew I wasn't was comfortable.

It wasn't that I was alone. There were a lot of Pervects on the street, and of course Kalvin was still with me. It's just that there is some company to which being alone is preferable. Kalvin's company was, of course, welcome ... which should narrow it down for even the most casual reader as to exactly what the source of my discomfort was.

The Pervects. (Very good! Move to the head of the class.) Now, saying one felt uncomfortable around Pervects may sound redundant. As has been noted, the entire dimension is not renowned for its sociability, much less its hospitality. What I learned on the streets that night, however, is that there are Pervects and there are Pervects.

Most of the natives I had dealt with up to this point had been just plain folk ... only nasty. In general, they seemed

61

to have jobs and were primarily concerned with making a living and looking out for themselves (not necessarily in that order). The ones populating the terrain after sunset, however, were of a different sort entirely.

Most noticeable were the ones sleeping in the doorways and gutters. At first, this struck me as a way to avoid paying a hundred a night for a room, and I said as much to Kalvin. He, in turn, suggested that I look a little closer at the Pervects who were sprawled about. I did, and consequently decided that *five* hundred in gold a night would not be too much to spend to avoid joining their ranks.

For openers, they were dirty . . . which probably isn't surprising if one sleeps in the gutter. While I've never claimed to have much of an eye for color, even in the poor light of the nighttime streets I could see that the green of their scales was an unhealthy hue. Frankly, they looked like something that was dead . . . only they weren't dead. I was to find out later, when I mentioned them to Edvik, that these were simply Pervects whose income had fallen below the dimensional standard of living. For whatever reason, they had gotten behind in the game, and now couldn't afford the lodgings and wardrobe to reestablish themselves.

Whatever financial problem the sleepers had encountered, they didn't have it in common with the Pervects who shared the night streets with them. Since they were primarily engaged in selling things, I'll refer to this second group as hustlers . . . even though doing so gives a negative connotation to that name I've never encountered before. While the daytime Pervects I had met might be described as "enterprising," the hustlers struck me more as "predatory."

They were as brightly dressed as any Imp, though they tended to hang back in the shadows, easing out to make muttered offers to passersby. What they were selling I was never sure, since none of them approached me directly. This is not to say they didn't notice my passing, for they watched me with flat reptilian eyes, but something in what they saw apparently convinced them to leave me alone. I can't say I was heartbroken by the omission.

I was so intent on watching the watchers I almost missed our restaurant. Kalvin spotted it, though, and after he'd brought it to my attention, we went in.

Way back when I first met Aahz, I had been exposed to a Pervish restaurant. Of course, that was at the Bazaar where there was an ordinance that Pervish restaurants had to have spells on them so they would keep moving around instead of lowering the property values by staying in one place, but it had still prepared me to a certain extent for what to expect.

Kalvin, on the other hand, had had no experience with Pervish eateries before. I almost lost him two steps into the place just from the smell. To be honest, I almost lost me, too. While I had been *exposed* to, I had never actually set foot *inside* one before. If there are those out there in a similar position to where I was experience-wise at this point, let me warn you: The smell loses a lot by the time it gets to the street.

"What died!?"

The Djin was holding his nose as he glanced disdainfully around the restaurant's interior.

"Come, come now, Kalvin," I said, trying to make light of the matter. "Haven't you ever smelled a good home-cooked meal before? You know, like mother used to burn?"

If the reader deduces from the foregoing that Pervish cooking is less than fragrant . . . that, perhaps, it stinks to high heaven, I can only say that my skill as a writer has finally reached the level of my readership. That is, indeed, what I have been attempting to say. Fortunately for the dimensions at large, however, mere words cannot convey the near-tangible texture of the stench.

"If my mother cooked like that, we would have gotten rid of her . . . even earlier than we did," Kalvin declared bluntly.

Curious comment, that.

"You can't tell me you *like* this," he insisted. "I mean, you may be a little strange, but you're still a sentient being."

"So are the Pervects."

"I'm willing to debate that . . . more than ever, now that I'm getting a feel for what they eat. You're avoiding the question, though. Are you really going to eat any of this stuff?"

I decided the joke had gone far enough.

"Not on a bet!" I admitted in a whisper. "If you watch closely, you'll see that some of the food actually crawls out of the bowl."

"I'd rather not!" Kalvin said, averting his eyes. "Seriously, Skeeve, if you aren't going to eat anything, why are we here?"

"Oh, I'm going to try to get something to eat. Just nothing they would prepare for the natives. That's why I was hunting for a place that served food from—and therefore, hopefully, stomachable by—off-world and off-worlders."

The Djin was unimpressed.

"I don't care *where* the recipe comes from. You're telling me you're going to take something that's been prepared in this kitchen and been in proximity with other dishes that stink the way these do, and then put it in your mouth? Maybe we should debate *your* qualifications as an intelligent being."

Looking at it that way, he had a point. Suddenly I didn't feel as clever as I had a few moments before.

"Cahn I help you, *sir*?"

The Pervect who materialized at my elbow was as stiffly formal as anything I'd seen that wasn't perched on a wedding cake. He had somehow mastered the technique of being subservient while still looking down on you. And they say that waiters can't be trained!

"Well, we . . . that is, I . . ."

"Ah! A Tah-bul for *one!*"

Actually, I had been preparing to beat a retreat, but this guy wasn't about to leave me that choice.

Chairs and tables seemed to part in his path as he swept off through the diners like a sailing ship through algae, drawing me along in his wake. Heads turned and murmurs started as we passed. If they were trying to figure out where they had seen me before, it could take a lot of talking.

"I wish I had thought to dress," I murmured to Kalvin. "This is a pretty classy place. I'm surprised they let me in without a tie."

The Djin shot me a look.

"I don't know how to say this, Skeeve, but you *are* dressed, and you *are* wearing a tie."

"Oh! Right."

I had forgotten I had altered my disguise spell in the taxi. One of the problems with the disguise spell is that I can't see the results myself. While I've gotten to a point where I can maintain the illusion without giving it a lot of conscious thought, it also means I occasionally forget what the appearance I'm maintaining really is.

I plopped down in the chair being held for me, but waved off the offered menu.

"I understand you serve dishes from off-dimension?"

The Pervect gave a little half-bow.

"Yas. Ve haff a wide selection for the most discriminating taste."

I nodded knowingly.

"Then just have the waiter bring me something Klahdish . . . and a decent wine to go with it."

"Very good, Sir."

He faded discreetly from view, leaving me to study our fellow diners. It was too much to hope that coincidence would lead Aahz to the same dining room, but it didn't hurt to look.

"You handled that pretty smoothly."

"What's that, Kalvin? Oh. The ordering. Thank you."

"Are you really that confident?"

I glanced around at the nearby tables for eavesdroppers before answering.

"I'm confident that I couldn't even read the menu," I said quietly. "Trying to fake it would only have made me look like a bigger fool. I just followed the general rule of 'When in doubt, rely on the waiter's judgment.' It usually works."

"True enough," Kalvin conceded. "But the waiter's not usually Pervish. It's still braver than I'd feel comfortable with, personally."

The Djin had a positive talent for making me feel uneasy about decisions that had already been made.

Fortunately, the wine arrived just then. I fidgeted through the tasting ritual, then started in drinking with a vengeance. A combination of nerves and thirst moved me rapidly through the first three glasses with barely a pause for breath.

"You might go a little easy on that stuff until you get some food in you," Kalvin advised pointedly.

"Not to worry," I waved. "One thing Aahz always told me: If you aren't sure of the food on a dimension, you can always drink your meals."

"He told you that, huh? What a buddy. Tell me, did it ever work?"

"Howzat?"

"Drinking your meals. Did it ever do you any good, or just land you in a lot of trouble?"

"Oh, we've had lots of trouble. Sometime lemme tell you about the time we decided to steal the trophy from the Big Game.

"You and Aahz?"

"No. Me and . . . um . . . it was . . ."

For some reason, I was having trouble remembering exactly who had been with me on that particular caper. I decided it might be wisest to get the subject of conversation off me until my meal arrived.

"Whoever. Speaking of bottles, though, how long had you been waiting before I pulled the cork on that one of yours?"

"Oh, not long for a Djin. In fact, I'd say it hadn't been more than . . ."

"Tananda!"

"Excuse me?"

"It was Tananda who was with me when we tried for the trophy . . . the first time, anyway."

"Oh."

"Glad that's off my back. Now, what was it you were saying, Kalvin?"

"Nothing important," the Djin shrugged.

He seemed a little distracted, but I thought I knew why.

"Kalvin, I'd like to apologize."

He seemed to relax a little.

"Oh, that's okay, Skeeve. It's just that . . ."

"No, I insist. It was rude of me to order without asking if you wanted something to eat, too. It's just that it would have been awkward trying to order food for someone no one else could see. Understand what I'm trying to say?"

"Of course."

I seemed to be losing him again.

"It wasn't that I had forgotten about you, really," I pressed. "I just thought that as small as you are, you wouldn't eat much and we could probably share my order. Now I can see that that's rather demeaning to you, so if you'd like your own order . . .''

"Sharing your meal will be fine. Okay? Can we drop the subject now?''

Whatever was bothering the Djin, my efforts to change his mood were proving woefully inadequate. I debated letting it go for the moment, but decided against it. Letting things go until later was how the situation with Aahz had gotten into its current state.

"Say . . . um . . . Kalvin?''

"Now what?''

"It's obvious that I've gotten you upset, and my trying to make amends is only making things worse. Now, it wasn't my intent to slight you in any way, but it seems to have happened anyway. If I can't make things better, can you at least tell me what it was I did so that I don't fall into the same trap again?''

"The wine doesn't help.''

I nodded at Kalvin's terse response. He was right. The wine was hitting me harder than I had expected, making it difficult to focus on him and what he was saying.

"It doesn't help . . . but that's not the whole problem,'' I said. "All alcohol does is amplify what's there already. It may make my irritating habits more irritating, but it isn't causing them.''

"True enough,'' he admitted grudgingly.

"So lay it on me,'' I urged. "What is it about me that's so irritating? I try to be a nice guy, but lately it hasn't been working so well. First with Aahz, and now with you.''

The Djin hesitated before answering.

"I haven't really known you all that long, Skeeve. Anything I could say would be a snap judgment.''

"So give me a snap judgment. I really want to . . .''

"Your dinner, Sir!"

The Pervect who had first seated me was hovering over my table again, this time with the waiter in tow. That latter notable was staggering under a huge covered platter which had steam rising from it enticingly.

I was desperately interested in hearing what Kalvin had to say, but the sight of the platter reminded me that I was desperately hungry as well. Apparently the Djin sensed my dilemma.

"Go ahead and eat, Skeeve," he said. "I can hold until you're done."

Nodding my thanks, I turned my attention to the waiting Pervect.

"It smells delicious," I managed, honestly surprised. "What is it?"

"Wan uf ze House Specialties," he beamed, reaching for the tray cover. "From Klah!"

The tray cover disappeared with a flourish, and I found myself face-to-face with someone else from my home dimension of Klah. Unfortunately, he wasn't serving the meal . . . he *was* the meal! Roasted, with a dead rat in his mouth as a garnish.

I did the only sane thing that occurred to me.

I fainted.

Chapter Eight:

"There's never a cop around when you need one!"

—A. CAPONE

"SKEEVE!"

The voice seemed to come from far away.

"C'mon, Skeeve! Snap out of it! We've got trouble!"

That caught my attention. I couldn't seem to get oriented, but if there was one thing I didn't need it was more trouble. *More* trouble? What . . . later! First, deal with whatever's going on now!

I forced my eyes open.

The scene which greeted me brought a lot of the situation back with a rush. I was in a restaurant . . . on the floor, to be specific . . . a Pervish waiter was hovering over me . . . and so was a policeman!

At first I thought it was the same one we had encountered earlier, but it wasn't. The similarities were enough that they could have come out of the same litter . . . or hatching. They both had the same square jaw, broad shoulders and potbelly, not to mention a very hard glint in their otherwise bored-looking eyes.

71

I struggled to sit upright, but wobbled as a wave of dizziness washed over me.

"Steady, Skeeve! You're going to need your wits about you for this one!"

Kalvin was hovering, his face lined with concern.

"W . . . what happened?" I said.

Too late I remembered that I was the only one who could see or hear the Djin. Ready or not, I had just opened the conversation with the others.

"It seems you fainted, boyo," the policeman supplied.

"I theenk he just does not vant to pay for zee food he ordered."

That was from the Pervect who had seated me, but his words brought it all back to me. The special dish from Klah!

"He served me a roast Klahd on a platter!" I said, leveling a shaky but accusing finger at the Pervect.

"Is that a fact now?"

The policeman cocked an eye at the Pervect, who became quite agitated.

"Non-sense! Eet is against the law to serve sentient beings without a li-cense. See for yourself, Offi-sair! Thees is a replica on-ley."

Sure enough, he was right! The figure on the platter was actually constructed on pieces of unidentifiable cuts of meat with what looked like baked goods filling in the gaps. The rat seemed to be authentic, but I'll admit I didn't look close. The overall effect was, as I can testify, horrifyingly real.

The policeman studied the dish closely before turning his attention to the waiter once more.

"Don't ya think it was a trifle harsh, servin' the lad with what seemed to be one of his own?"

"But he deed not look like thees when he came in! I on-ley served heem what he asked for . . . sometheeng from Klah!"

That's when I became aware of the fact that my disguise spell was no longer on. I must have lost control of it when I fainted. When it disappeared, however, was not as important as the fact that it was gone! I was now seen by one and all as what I really was . . . a Klahd!

The policeman had now turned his gaze on me and was studying me with what I felt was unhealthy interest.

"Really, now," he said. "Perhaps you could be tellin' how it is you come to be wearin' a disguise in such a fine place? It couldn't be that you were plannin' to skip out without payin' fer yer meal, could it?"

"No. It's just that . . . ," I paused as a wave of dizziness passed. "Well, I've heard you can get better service and prices on Perv if folks don't know you're from off-dimension."

"Bad answer, Skeeve," Kalvin hissed, but I had already figured that out.

The policeman had gone several shades darker, and his head almost disappeared into his neck. Though his tone was still cordial, he seemed to be picking his words very carefully.

"Are ya tryin' to tell me you think our whole dimension is full of clip joints and thieves? Is that what yer sayin'?"

Too late I saw my error. Aahz had always seemed to be proud of the fact that Pervects were particularly good at turning a profit. It had never occurred to me that to some, this might sound like an insult.

"Not at all," I said hastily. "I assumed it was like any other place . . . that the best prices and services were reserved for locals and visitors got what was left. I was just trying to take advantage of normal priorities, that's all."

I thought it was a pretty good apology. The policeman, however, seemed unimpressed. Unsmiling, he produced a notepad and pencil.

"Name?"

His voice was almost flat and impersonal, but managed to still convey a degree of annoyance.

"Look. I'll pay for the meal, if that's what the problem is."

"I didn't ask if you were payin' for the meal. I asked you what your name is. Now are you going to tell me here, or should we be talkin' down at the precinct station?"

Kalvin was suddenly hovering in front of me again.

"Better tell him, Skeeve," he said, his tone matching his worried expression. "This cop seems to have an Eath up his Yongie."

That one threw me.

"A what up his what?"

The policeman looked up from his notepad.

"And how are ya spellin' that, now?"

"Umm . . . forget it. Just put down 'Skeeve.' That's my name."

His pencil moved briskly, and for a moment I thought I had gotten away with my gaffe. No such luck.

" . . . And what was that you were sayin' before?"

"Oh, nothing. Just a nickname."

Even to me, the explanation sounded weak. Kalvin groaned as the policeman gave me a hard look before scribbling a few more notes on his pad.

"An alias, is it?" he murmured under his breath.

This was sounding worse all the time.

"But . . . "

"Residence?"

"The New Inn."

My protests seemed to be only making things worse, so I resolved to answer any other questions he might have as simply and honestly as possible.

"A hotel, eh?" The pencil was moving faster now. "And

where would your regular residence be?"

"The Bazaar at Deva."

The policeman stopped writing. Raising his hand, he peered at me carefully.

"Now I thought we had gotten this matter of disguises settled," he said, a bit too casually. "So tell me, Mr. Skeeve, are you a Klahd . . . or a Deveel masquerading as one?"

"I'm a Klahd . . . really!"

" . . . Who lives on Deva," the policeman finished grimly. "That's a pretty expensive place to be callin' home, boyo. Just what is it you do for a livin' that you can afford such an extravagant address . . . or to pay for expensive meals you aren't going to eat, for that matter?"

"I uh, work for a corporation . . . M.Y.T.H. Inc. . . . It's a co-op of magik consultants."

"Is that a fact?" The policeman's skepticism was open. "Tell me, boyo, what is it you do for them that they had to hire a Klahd instead of one of their local lads?"

Maybe I was recovering from passing out, or maybe his sarcasm was getting to me, but I started to get a bit annoyed with the questions.

"I'm the president *and* founder," I snapped, "and since I personally recruited the staff, they didn't have whole bunches to say about my qualifications."

Actually, they had had a lot to say. Specifically, they were the ones who railroaded me into my current lofty position. Somehow, though, this didn't seem to be the time to try to point that out.

"Really?" The policeman was still pushing, but he seemed a lot more respectful now. "It's clear that there's more to you than meets the eye, *Mister* Skeeve."

"Steady, Skeeve," the Djin said quietly. "Let's not get too aggressive with the representatives of the local law."

It was good advice, and I tried to get a handle on my temper.

"You can check it out if you like," I said stiffly.

"Oh, I intend to. Would you mind tellin' me what the president of a corporation from Deva is doin' in our fair dimension? Are you here on business?"

"Well . . . I guess you could say that."

"Good. Then I'm sure you won't mind givin' me the names of our citizens you're dealin' with."

Too late I saw the trap. As a businessman, I should have local references. This may seem like a silly oversight to you, but you'll have to remember my background up to this point. Most of my ventures into the various dimensions have been more of the raider or rescue mission variety, so it never occurred to me there was another way of doing business. Of course, admitting this would probably do little toward improving the impression I was making on this stalwart of the law.

I considered my alternatives. I considered trying to lie my way out of the predicament. Finally, I decided to give the truth one last try.

"There isn't anyone specifically that I'm dealing with." I said carefully. "The fact of the matter is that I'm looking for someone."

"Oh? Then you're hirin' for your corporation? Out to raid some of our local talent?"

That didn't sound too good either.

"It's not a recruiting mission, I assure you. I'm trying to find my . . . one of our employees."

The policeman straightened a bit, looking up from his notebook once more.

"Now, that's a different matter entirely," he said. "Have you been by a station to fill out a missing person report?"

I tried to imagine Aahz's reaction if I had the police pick

him up. Mercifully, my mind blocked the image.

"Are you kidding? I mean . . . no, I haven't."

" . . . Or do you think you're better at locatin' folks than the police are?"

I was getting desperate. It seemed that no matter what I said, it was getting twisted into the worst possible interpretation.

"He's not really missing. Look, officer, I had a falling out with my old partner, who happens to also be the co-founder of the corporation *and* a Pervect. He left in a huff, presumably to return here to Perv. All I want to do is locate him and try to convince him to come back to the company, or at least make amends so we can part on more agreeable terms. In short, while it's business related, it's more of a personal matter."

The policeman listened intently until I had finished.

"Well, why didn't you say so in the first place, lad?" he scowled, flipping his notebook shut. "I'll have you know my time's too valuable to be wastin' chattin' with everybody who wants to tell me his life story."

"Nice going, Skeeve!" Kalvin winked, flashing me a high sign. "I think we're off the hook."

I ignored him. The policeman's comment about wasting his time had reignited my irritation. After all, he had been the one who had prolonged the interrogation.

"Just a moment," I said, as he started to turn away. "Does this mean you won't be running that check on me?"

"Skeeve!" the Djin warned, but it was too late.

"Is there any reason I shouldn't?" the policeman said, turning back to me again.

"It's just that you've taken up so much of your valuable time asking questions about a simple fainting, I'd hate to see you waste any more."

"Now don't go tryin' to tell me how to do my job, *Mister*

Skeeve,'' he snarled, pushing his face close to mine. ''Fer yer information, I'm not so sure this is as simple as you try to cut it out to be.''

''It isn't?''

That last snappy response of mine was sort of squeaked out. I was suddenly aware that I was not as far out of the woods as I had believed.

''No, it isn't. We have what seems to be a minor disturbance in a public restaurant, only the person at the center of it turns out to be travelin' in disguise. What's more, he's from off-dimension and used to usin' aliases, and even though he claims to be an honest businessman, there doesn't seem to be anyone locally who can vouch for him, or any immediate way of confirmin' his story. Now doesn't that strike you as bein' a little suspicious?''

''Well, if you put it that way . . . ''

''I do! However, as I was sayin', we're pretty busy down at the station, and for all yer jabberin' you *seem* harmless enough, so I don't see much point to pursuin' this further. Just remember, I've got you down in my book, boyo, and if there's any trouble you'll find I'm not so understandin' next time!''

With that, he turned on his heel and marched out of the restaurant.

''That was close,'' Kalvin whistled. ''You shouldn't have mouthed off that last time.''

I had arrived at much the same conclusion, but nodded my agreement anyway.

The waiter was still hovering about, so I signaled him for our check. The last thing I needed to do now would be to forget and try to walk out without paying.

''So where do we go from here?'' the Djin asked.

''I think we'll settle up here and head back to the hotel for some sleep. Two run-ins with the police in one day is about all the excitement I can handle.''

"But you haven't eaten anything.''

"I'll do it tomorrow. Like I said, I don't relish the thought of risking another brush with the law . . . even accidentally.''

Despite his advice to go easy with the police, the Djin seemed unconcerned.

"Don't worry. So far it's been just talk. I mean, what can they do to you? There's no law against being polite on the sidewalk or fainting in a restaurant.''

"They could run that check on me. I'm not wild about having the police poking around in my affairs.''

The Djin gave me a funny look.

"So what if they do? I mean, it's annoying, but nothing to worry about. It's not like you have a criminal record or have connections with organized crime or anything.''

I thought about Don Bruce and the Mob. Suddenly, my work with them didn't seem as harmless as it had when I first agreed to take the position as the Mob's representative on Deva. Fortunately, no one on Deva except my own crew was aware of it, and they weren't likely to talk. Still, with the way my luck had been running lately, there was no point in risking a police check. Also, I could see no point in worrying Kalvin by letting him know what kind of a powder keg I might be sitting on.

Chapter Nine:

" . . . You gotta start somewhere."
                                    —S. McDUCK

I HAD PLANNED to sleep late the next morning. I mean, I was eager to locate Aahz and all that, but it was rare that I had the opportunity to lounge in bed a couple extra hours. Business had been brisk enough that I usually headed into the offices early to try to get some work done before the daily parade of questions and problems started. Even when I did decide to try to sleep in, the others would be up and about, so I felt pressured to rise and join in for fear I might be excluded from an important or interesting conversation. Consequently, now that I had a chance to laze about I fully intended to take advantage of it. Besides, between the restaurant and the police it had been a rough night.

Unfortunately, it seemed the rest of the world had different ideas about my sleeping habits.

I had had trouble dozing off anyway, what with the unaccustomed traffic noise and all. When I did finally manage to get to sleep, it seemed I had barely closed my eyes when there was a brisk knocking at the door of my room.

"Wazzit?" I called, struggling to get my eyes open far enough to navigate.

In response, the door opened and the bellhop who had brought my luggage up the day before came bustling into the room.

"Sorry to bother you so early, Mr. Skeeve, but there's . . . "

He stopped abruptly and peered around the room. I was still trying to figure out what he was looking for when he returned his attention to me once more.

"Mr. Skeeve?" he said again, his voice as hesitant as his manner.

"Yes?" I responded, trying to hold my annoyance in check. "You had something to tell me? Something I assume couldn't wait until a decent hour?"

If I had hoped to rebuff him, I failed dismally. At the sound of my voice his face brightened and he relaxed visibly.

"So it *is* you. You had me going there for a minute. You've changed since you checked in."

It took me a second to realize what he was talking about. Then I remembered I hadn't renewed my disguise spell since I had my run-in with the law the night before. I suppose it could be a little jarring to expect to find a Pervect and end up talking to a Klahd instead. I considered casting the spell again, then made a snap decision to leave things the way they were. The Pervect disguise seemed to be causing me more trouble than it was averting. I'd try it for a day as a Klahd and see how things went.

"Disguise," I said loftily. "What is it?"

"Well, there's . . . Is *this* the disguise or was the other?"

"This is the real me, if it matters. Now what is it?"

"Oh, it doesn't matter to me. We get folks from all sorts of strange dimensions here at the hotel. I always say, it doesn't matter where they're from, as long as their gold is . . . ''

"WHAT IS IT??"

I have found that my tolerance for small talk moves in a direct ratio to how long I've been awake, and today was proving to be no exception.

"Oh, sorry. There's a cabbie downstairs in the loading zone who says he's waiting for you. I thought you'd like to know."

I felt the operative word there was "waiting," but it seemed to have escaped the bellhop entirely. Still, I was awake now, and my search wasn't going to get any shorter if I just sat around my room.

"Okay. Tell him I'll be down in a few minutes."

"Sure thing. Oh . . . the other thing I wanted to ask you . . . Is it okay if this guy Aahz finds out you're looking for him?"

I had to think about that for a few moments. Aahz had left without talking to me, but I didn't think he was avoiding me to a point where he'd go into hiding if he knew I was on Perv.

"That shouldn't be a problem. Why?"

"I was thinking of running an ad in the personal section of the newspaper, but then it occurred to me that he might owe you money or something, so I thought I'd better check first."

"The personal section?"

"It's a daily bulletin board the paper prints," Kalvin supplied as he joined us in mid-yawn. "Notes from people to people . . . birthday greetings, messages from wives to wayward husbands, that sort of thing. A lot of people read them faithfully."

Somehow that didn't sound like Aahz's cup of tea, but

there was always a chance that someone who knew him would see it and pass on the information. In any case, it couldn't hurt.

"Oh, right. The personal ads. Sorry, I'm still waking up. Sounds like a good idea," I said, rummaging around for some loose change. "How much does it cost?"

To my surprise, the bellhop held up a restraining hand.

"I'll go the cost on my own if you don't mind, Mr. Skeeve."

"Oh?"

"Sure. That way, if it works, there won't be any doubt who gets that reward you mentioned."

With that, he flashed me a quick grin and left. It occurred to me that I should start watching my spending to be sure I'd have enough to actually pay a reward if the bellhop or one of his friends managed to locate Aahz for me.

"So what's the plan for today, Skeeve?"

Kalvin followed me into the bathroom and asked his question as I was peering at my face in the mirror. Things were getting to a point where I had to shave, but only occasionally . . . and I decided today wasn't one of those occasions. It's funny, when I was younger I used to look forward to shaving, but now that it was fast upon me I tended to see it as the nuisance it was. I began to understand why some men grew beards.

"Well, I don't think we should just sit around here waiting for Aahz to answer the bellhop's personal ad," I said. "Besides, it won't produce any results today, anyway. I figure we should do a little looking on our own."

As soon as I said it, I realized how simplistic that sounded. Of course we were going to go looking for Aahz. That's what we would have done if the bellhop hadn't come up with his "personal ad" idea. If Kalvin noticed, however, he let me get away with it.

"Sounds good to me. Where do we start?"

I had been giving that some thought. Unfortunately, the end result was that I was embarrassed to realize how little I knew about Aahz's background . . . or the background of any of my other colleagues, for that matter.

"The main things Aahz seems to specialize in are magik and finances. I thought we'd poke around those circles a while and see if anyone can give us a lead."

As it turned out, however, there was one small episode which delayed the start of our quest.

We had just stepped out of the doors of the hotel and were looking around for Edvik when I noticed the street vendors. They had been there the day before when we checked in, but I had failed to really notice or comment on them. Today, however, they caught my attention, if for no other reason than their contrast to the hustlers who populated the same area at night.

The night hustlers were an intense, predatory lot who seemed willing to trade for *some* of your money only if they felt like they couldn't simply knock you down and take it *all* directly. The day people, on the other hand, seemed to be more like low-budget retailers who stood quietly behind their makeshift briefcase stands or blankets and smiled or made their pitches to any passersby who chanced to pause to look at their displays. If anything, their manner was furtive rather than sinister, and they kept glancing up and down the street as if they were afraid of being observed at their trade.

"I wonder what they're watching for?" I said, almost to myself. I say almost because I forgot for the moment that Kalvin was hovering within easy hearing.

"Who? Them? They're probably watching for the police."

"The police? Why?"

"For the usual reason . . . what they're doing is illegal."

"It is?"

I had no desire to have another run-in with the police, but I was genuinely puzzled. Maybe I was missing something, but I couldn't see anything untoward about the street vendors' activities.

"I keep forgetting. You're from the Bazaar at Deva," the Djin laughed. "You see, Skeeve, unlike the Bazaar, most places require a license to be a street vendor. From the look of them, these poor souls can't afford one. If they could, they'd probably open a storefront instead of working the street."

"You mean this is it for them? They aren't distributing for a larger concern?"

On Deva, most of the street vendors were employees of larger businesses who picked up their wares in the morning and returned what was unsold at the end of their shift. Their specific strategy was to look like a small operation so that tourists who were afraid of dickering at a storefront or tent would buy, assuming they knew more and could get better prices from a lowly street peddler. It never occurred to me that the street vendors I had been seeing really were small, one-person operations.

"That's right," Kalvin was saying. "What you see is what you get. Most of those people have their life savings tied up in . . . Hey! Where are you going?"

I ignored him, stepping boldly up to one of the vendors I *had* noticed the day before. He was in the same spot as yesterday, squatting behind a blanket full of sunglasses and cheap bracelets. What had caught my eye yesterday was that he was young, even younger than I was. Considering the longevity of Pervects, that made him very young indeed.

"See anything you like?" he said, flashing an expanse

of pointed teeth I would have found unnerving if I hadn't gotten used to Aahz's grins.

"Actually, I was hoping you could answer a few questions for me."

The smile disappeared.

"What are you? A reporter or something?"

"No. Just curious."

He scowled and glanced around.

"I suppose it's all right, as long as it doesn't interfere with any paying customers. Time's money, ya know."

In response, I tossed a gold coin into his blanket.

"So call me a customer who's buying some of your time. Let me know when that's used up."

He made a quick pass with his hand and the coin disappeared as his smile emerged from hiding.

"Mister, you just got my attention. Ask your questions."

"Why do you do this?"

The smile faded into a grimace.

"Because I'm independently wealthy and get my kicks sitting in the rain and running from the cops . . . why do you think? I do it for the money, same as everybody else."

"No. I meant why do you do *this* for money instead of getting a job?"

He studied me for a moment with his Pervish yellow eyes, then gave a small shrug.

"All right," he said. "I'll give you a straight answer. You don't get rich working for someone else . . . especially not at the kind of jobs I'd been qualified for. You see, I don't come from money. All my folks gave me was my name. After that I was pretty much on my own. I don't have much school to my credit, and, like I say, my family isn't connected. I can't get a good job from an old pal of my dad's. That means I'd start at the bottom . . . and probably end there, too. Anyway, I gave it a good long think, and decided I wanted more out of life.''

I tried to think of a tactful way of saying that this still looked pretty bottom of the barrel to me.

'' . . . So you think this is better than working at an entry-level job for someone else?''

His head came up proudly.

''I didn't say that. I don't figure to be doing this forever. This is just a way to raise the capital to start a bigger business. I'm risking it all on my own abilities. If it works, I get all the profits instead of a wage and I can move on to better things. What's more, if it works well enough, I've got more to pass on to my kids than my parents did. If it doesn't . . . well, I'm no worse off than when I started.''

''You've got kids?''

''Who, me? No . . . at least, not yet. Maybe someday. Right now, the way things are going, I can't even afford a steady girlfriend, if you know what I mean.''

Actually, I didn't. I had plenty of money personally, but no girlfriend. Therefore, I didn't have the vaguest idea what the upkeep on one would be.

''Well, I'd say it's a noble cause you have there . . . wanting to build something to leave for your kids.''

At that he laughed, flashing those teeth again.

''Don't try to make me sound too good,'' he said. ''I won't kid you. I'd like a few of the nicer things in life myself . . . like staying at fancy hotels and driving around in cabs. I'd use up some of the profits before I passed them on to my kids.''

I was suddenly aware of the differences in our economic standing . . . that what he was dreaming about I tended to take for granted. The awareness made me uncomfortable.

''Yeah . . . well, I've got to be going now. Oh! What was it, anyway?''

"What was what?"

"The name your parents gave you."

"It wasn't that hot, really," he said, making a face. "My friends just call me J. R."

With that, I beat a hasty retreat to my waiting cab.

"What was that all about?" Edvik said as I sank back into my seat.

"Oh, I was just curious about what made the street vendors tick."

"Them? Why bother? They're just a bunch of low-life hustlers scrabbling for small change. They're never going to get anywhere."

I was surprised at the sudden vehemence in his voice. There was clearly no love lost there.

It occurred to me that Edvik's appraisal of the street vendors pretty much summed up my initial reaction to his own enterprising efforts with his cab and self-publishing company.

It also occurred to me, as I reflected on my conversation with J. R., that I had been even more lucky than I had realized when I had taken to studying magik . . . first with Garkin and then with Aahz. It didn't take the wildest stretching of the imagination to picture myself in the street vendor's place . . . assuming I had that much initiative to begin with.

All in all, it wasn't a particularly comforting thought.

Chapter Ten:

"All financiers are not created equal!"
        —R. CORMAN

"SO WHERE ARE we off to today, Mr. Skeeve?"

Edvik's words interrupted my thoughts, and I fought to focus my attention on the problem at hand.

"Either to talk with the magicians or some financial types," I said. "I was hoping that as our trusty native guide you'd have some ideas as to which to hit first . . . and it's just 'Skeeve,' not 'Mr. Skeeve.' "

The "Mr. Skeeve" thing had been starting to get to me with the bellhop, but it hadn't seemed worth trying to correct. If I was going to be spending the next few days traveling with Edvik, however, I thought I'd try to set him straight before he got on my nerves.

"All right. Skeeve it is," the cabbie agreed easily. "Just offhand, I'd say it would probably be easier to start with the financial folks."

That hadn't been what I had hoped he'd say, but as I've noted before, there's no point in paying for guidance and then not following it.

"Okay. I'll go along with that. Any particular reason, though?"

"Sure. First of all, there are a lot of people in the magik business around here. We got schools, consultants, co-ops, entertainers, weather control and home defense outfits . . . all sorts. What's more, they're spread out all over. We could spend the next year trying to check them out and still have barely scratched the surface. There aren't nearly as many financiers, on the other hand, so if they're on your list I figured we could start with them. Maybe we'll get lucky and not have to deal with the magik types."

I was a little staggered by his casual recitation. The enormity of what I was trying to do was just starting to sink in. I had only allowed a week to find Aahz and convince him to come back. At the moment, it seemed next to impossible to accomplish that in so short a time, yet I couldn't take any longer with the rest of the crew taking on Queen Hemlock without me. With an effort, I tried to put my doubts out of my mind. At the very least, I had to try. I'd face up to what to do next at the end of the week . . . not before.

"What's the other reason?"

"Excuse me?"

"You said 'First of all. . . .' That usually implies there's more than one reason."

The cabbie shot me a glance over his shoulder.

"That's right. Well, if you must know, I'm a little uncomfortable around magicians . . . current company excepted, of course. Never had much call to deal with 'em and just as happy to keep it that way. I've got a buddy, though, who's a financier. He just might be able to help you out. Most of these finance types know each other, you know. Leastwise, I can probably get you in to see him without an appointment."

Kalvin was waving a hand at me, trying to get my attention.

"I probably don't have to remind you of this," he said, "but your time *is* rather limited. I didn't say anything about your chatting with that scruffy street vendor, but are you really going to blow off part of a day talking to a supposed financier who hangs out with cab drivers?"

"How did you meet this guy?" I queried, trying desperately to ignore the Djin's words . . . or, to be exact, how closely they echoed my own thoughts.

"Oh, we sort of ran into each other at an art auction."

"An art auction?"

I didn't mean to let my incredulity show in my voice, but it kind of slipped out. In response, Edvik twisted around in his seat to face me directly.

"Yeah. An auction. What's the matter? Don't you think I can appreciate art?"

Left to their own devices, the lizards powering our vehicle began veering toward the curb.

"Well . . . no. I mean, I've never met an art collector before. I don't know much about art, so it surprised me, that's all. No offense," I said hurriedly, trying not to tense as the cab wandered back and forth in our lane.

"You asked. That's where we met."

The cabbie returned his attention to the road once more, casually bringing us back on course.

"Were you both bidding on the same painting?"

"No. He offered to back half my bid so I could stay in the running . . . only it wasn't a painting. It was more what you would call literary."

Now I was getting confused.

"Literary? But I thought you said it was an art auction."

"It was, but there was an author there who offered to

auction off an appearance in his next book. Well, I knew
the author . . . I had done an interview with him in one of
the 'zines I publish . . . so I thought it would be kind of
neat to see how he would do me in print. Anyway, it came
down to two of us, and the bidding got pretty stiff. I thought
I was going to have to drop out.''

"That's when the financier offered to back your bid?''

"Actually, he made the offer to the other guy first. Lucky
for me the other bidder wanted the appearance for his wife,
so he wouldn't go along with the deal. That's when the
Butterfly turned to me.''

"Wait a minute. The Butterfly?''

"That's what he calls himself. It's even on his business
cards. Anyway, if he hadn't come in on the bid, you'd be
spending a couple chapters talking to some guy's winsome
but sexy wife instead of . . . ''

At that point I was listening with only half an ear as
Edvik prattled on. A financier named Butterfly who backs
cabbies' bids at auctions. I didn't have to look at Kalvin to
tell the Djin was rolling his eyes in an anguished "I told
you so.'' Still, the more I thought about it, the more hopeful
I became. This Butterfly just might be offbeat enough to
know something about Aahz. I figured it was at least worth
a try.

Strange as it may sound, I was as nervous about meeting
the Butterfly as Edvik claimed to be about dealing with
magicians. Magicians I had been dealing with for several
years and knew what to expect . . . or if my experiences
were an accurate sample, what *not* to expect. Financiers,
on the other hand, were a whole different kettle of fish. I
had no idea what I was getting into or how to act. I tried
to reassure myself by remembering that this particular financier had dealt with Edvik in the past, and so could not be

too stuffy. Still, I found myself straightening my disguise spell nervously as the cabbie called up to the Butterfly from the lobby. I was still traveling as a Klahd, but had used my disguise spell to upgrade my wardrobe a bit so that I at least *looked* like I was comfortable in monied circles.

I needn't have worried.

The Butterfly did not live up to any of my preconceived notions or fears about what a financier was like. First of all, instead of an imposing office lined with shelves full of leatherbound books and incomprehensible charts, it seemed he worked out of his apartment, which proved to be smaller than my own office, though much more tastefully furnished. Secondly, he was dressed quite casually in a pair of slacks and a pastel-colored sweater, that actually made me feel uncomfortably overdressed in my disguise-spell generated suit. Fortunately, his manner itself was warm and friendly enough to put me at my ease almost immediately.

"Pleased to meet you . . . Skeeve, isn't it?" he said, extending a hand for a handshake.

"Yes. I . . . I'm sorry to impose on your schedule like this . . ."

"Nonsense. Glad to help. That's why I'm self-employed . . . so I can control my own schedule. Please. Have a seat and make yourself at home."

Once we were seated, however, I found myself at a loss as to how I should begin the conversation. But, with the Butterfly watching me with attentive expectation, I felt I had to say something.

"Um . . . Edvik tells me you met at an art auction?"

"That's right . . . though I'll admit that for me it was more of a whim than anything else. Edvik is really much more the collector and connoisseur than I am."

The cabbie preened visibly under the implied praise.

"No. I just dropped by out of curiosity. I had heard that

this particular auction had a reputation for being a lot of
fun, so I pulled a couple thousand out of the bank and
wandered in to see for myself. The auctioneers were amus-
ing, and the bidding was lively, but most of the art being
offered didn't go with my current decor. So when that one
particular item came up . . .''

I tried to keep an interested face on, but my mind wasn't
on his oration. Instead, I kept pondering the easy way he
had said '' . . . so I pulled a couple thousand . . .'' Clearly
this was a different kind of Pervect than Aahz was. My old
partner would have been more willing to casually part with
a couple pints of his blood than with gold.

'' . . . But in the long run it worked out fine.''

The Butterfly was finishing his tale, and I laughed duti-
fully along with him.

''Tell him about your friend, Skeeve.''

''That's right. Here I've been rattling on and we haven't
even started to address your problem,'' the financier nodded,
shifting forward on his chair. ''Edvik said you were trying
to locate someone who might have been active in our financial circles.''

''I'm not sure you'll be able to help,'' I began, grateful
for not having to raise the subject myself. ''He's been off-
dimension for several years now. His name is Aahz.''

The Butterfly pursed his lips thoughtfully.

''The name doesn't ring any bells. Of course, in these
days of nesting corporations and holding companies, names
don't really mean much. Can you tell me anything about
his style?''

''His style?''

''How would you describe his approach to money? Is he
a plunger? A dabbler?''

I had to laugh at that.

''Well, the words 'tight-fisted' and 'penny-pinching' are the first that come to mind.''

''There's 'tight-fisted' and there's 'cautious,' '' the Butterfly smiled. ''Perhaps you'd better tell me a little about him, and let me try to extract and analyze the pertinent parts.''

So I told him. Once I had gotten started, the words seemed to come rushing out in a torrent.

I told him about meeting Aahz when he got stranded on my home dimension of Klah after a practical joke gone awry robbed him of his magikal powers, and how he took me on as an apprentice after we stymied Isstvan's plan to take over the dimensions. I told him about how Aahz had convinced me to try out for the position of Court Magician for the kingdom of Possiltum, and how that had led to our confrontation with Big Julie's army as well as introducing me to the joys of bureaucratic in-fighting. He clucked sympathetically when I told him about how Tananda and I had tried to steal the trophy from the Big Game as a birthday present for Aahz, and how we had had to put together a team to challenge the two existing teams after Tananda got caught. He was amused by my rendition of how I got stuck masquerading as Roderick, the king, and how I got Massha as an apprentice, though he seemed most interested in the part about how we broke up the Mob's efforts to move into the Bazaar at Deva and ended up working for both sides of the same brawl. I even told him about our brief sortie into Limbo when Aahz got framed for murdering a vampire, and my even briefer career into the arena of professional Dragon Poker which pitted my friends and me against the Sen-Sen Ante Kid and the Ax. Finally, I tried to explain how we expanded our operation into a corporation, ending with how Aahz had walked out, leaving a note behind stating that, without his powers, he felt he was needless baggage to the group.

The Butterfly listened to it all, and, when I finally ground to a halt, he remained motionless for many long minutes, apparently digesting what he had heard.

"Well, one thing I can tell you," he said at last. "Your friend isn't a financier . . . here on Perv, or anywhere else, for that matter."

"He isn't? But he's always talking about money."

"Oh, there's more to being a financier than talking about money," the Butterfly laughed. "The whole idea is to put one's money to work through investments. If anything, this Aahz's hoarding techniques would indicate that he's pretty much an amateur when it comes to money. You, on the other hand, by incorporating and diversifying through holdings in other businesses, show marked entrepreneurial tendencies. Perhaps sometime we might talk a bit about mutual investment opportunities."

I suppose it was all quite flattering, and under other circumstances I might have been happy to chat at length with the Butterfly about money management. Unfortunately, I couldn't escape the disappointment of the bottom line . . . that he wouldn't be able to give me any information that would help me locate Aahz.

"Thanks, but right now I think I'd better focus on one thing at a time, and my current priority is finding my old partner."

"Well, sorry I couldn't have been of more assistance," the financier said, rising to his feet. "One thing, though, Skeeve, if you don't mind a little advice?"

"What's that?"

"You might try to take a bit more of an active role in your own life. You know . . . instead of reactive?"

That one stopped me short as I was reaching for the door.

"Excuse me?"

"Nothing. It was just a thought."

"Well, could you elaborate a little? C'mon, Butterfly! Don't drop a line like that on me without some kind of an explanation to go with it."

"It's really none of my business," he shrugged, "but I couldn't help but notice during your story that you seemed to be living your life reacting to crisis rather than having any real control over things. Your old partner and mentor got dropped in your lap and the two of you teamed up to stop someone who might try to assassinate either of you next. It was Aahz who forced you to try for the job as court magician, and ever since then you've been yielding to pressure, real or perceived, from almost everybody in your life: Tananda, Massha, the Mob, the Devan Chamber of Commerce . . . even whatzisname, Grimble and that Badaxe have leaned on you. It just seems to me that for someone as successful as you obviously are, you really haven't shown much gumption or initiative."

His words hit me like a bucket of cold water. I had been shouted out by experts, but somehow Butterfly's calm criticism cut me deeper than any tonguelashing I had ever recieved from Aahz.

"Things have been kind of scrambled . . . " I started, but the financier cut me off.

"I can see that, and I don't mean to tell you how to run your life. You've had some strong-willed, dominating people who have been doing just that, though, and I'd have to say the main offender has been this fellow, Aahz. Now, I know you're concerned about your friendship, but if I were you, I'd think long and hard about inviting him back into my life until I had gotten my own act together."

Chapter Eleven:

"How come I get all the hard questions?"
                                    —O. NORTH

"SKEEVE! HEY, SKEEVE! Can ya ease up for a bit?"

The words finally penetrated my self-imposed fog and I slackened my pace, letting Kalvin catch up with me.

"Whew! Thanks," the Djin said, hovering in his now-accustomed place. "I told you before I'm not real strong. Even hovering takes energy, ya know. You were really moving there."

"Sorry," I responded curtly, more out of habit than anything else.

In all honesty, the Djin's comfort was not a high priority item in my mind just then. I had had Edvik drive us back to the hotel after we left the Butterfly's place. Instead of going on up to my room, however, I had headed off down the sidewalk. The street vendor I had spoken to earlier waved a friendly greeting, but I barely acknowledged it with a curt nod of my head. The Butterfly's observations on my life had loosed an explosion of thoughts in my mind, and I figured maybe a brisk walk would help me sort things out.

I don't know how long I walked before Kalvin's plea snapped me out of my mental wheel-spinning. I had only vague recollections of shouldering my way past slower-moving pedestrians and snarling at those who were quick enough to get out of my path on their own. The police would have been pleased to witness it . . . only on Perv two days and already I could walk down the street like a native.

"Look, do you want to talk about this? Maybe some place sitting down?"

I looked closer at the Djin. He really did look tired, his face streaked with sweat and his little chest heaving as he tried to catch his breath. Strange, I didn't feel like I had been exerting myself at all.

"Talk about what?" I said, realizing as I spoke that the words were coming out forced and tense.

"Come on, Skeeve. It's obvious that what the Butterfly said back there has you upset. I don't know why, it sounded like pretty good advice to me, but maybe talking it out would help a bit."

"Why should I be upset?" I snapped. "He only challenged all the priorities I've been living by and suggested that my best friend is probably the worst thing in my life. Why should that bother me?"

"It shouldn't," Kalvin responded innocently, "unless, of course, he's right. Then I could see why it *would* bother you."

I opened my mouth for an angry retort, then shut it again. I really couldn't think of anything to say. The Djin had just verbalized my worst fears, ones I didn't have any answers for.

" . . . And running away from it won't help! You're going to have to face up to it before you're any good to yourself . . . or anyone else, for that matter."

Kalvin's voice came from behind me, and I realized I had picked up my pace again. At the same moment, I saw that he was right, I was trying to run away from the issues, both figuratively and literally. With that knowledge, the fatigue of my mental and physical efforts hit me all at once and I sagged, slowing to a stop on the sidewalk.

"That's better. Can we talk now?"

"Sure. Why not? I feel like getting something in my stomach, anyway."

The Djin gave a theatrical wince.

"Ootch! You mean we're going to try to find a restaurant again? Remember what happened the last time?"

In spite of myself I had to smile at his antics.

"As a matter of fact, I was thinking more on the order of getting something to drink."

While I spoke, I was casting about for a bar. One thing about Perv I had noticed, you never seemed to be out of sight of at least one establishment that served alcoholic beverages. This spot proved to be no exception, and now that I was more attuned to my environment, I discovered just such a place right next to where we were standing.

"This looks like as good a spot as any," I said, reaching for the door. "C'mon, Kalvin, I'll buy the first round."

It was meant as a joke, because I hadn't seen the Djin eat or drink anything since I released him from the bottle. He seemed quite agitated at the thought, however, hanging back instead of moving with me.

"Wait, Skeeve, I don't think we should . . ."

I didn't dally to hear the rest. What the heck, this *had* been his idea . . . sort of. Fighting a sudden wave of irritation, I pushed on into the bar's interior.

At first glance, the place looked a little seedy. Also the second and third glances, though it took a moment for my eyes to adjust to the dim light. It was small, barely big

enough to hold the half-dozen tiny tables that crowded the
floor. Sagging pictures and clippings adorned the walls,
though what they were about specifically I couldn't tell
through the grime obscuring their faces. There was a small
bar with stools along one wall, where three tough-looking
patrons crouched hunched forward in conversation with the
bartender. They ceased talking and regarded me briefly with
cold, unfriendly stares as I surveyed the place, though
whether their hostility was because I was a stranger or because I was from off-dimension I wasn't sure. It did occur
to me that I was still wearing my disguise spell business
suit which definitely set me apart from the dark, weather-
beaten outfits the other patrons wore almost like a uniform.
It also occurred to me that this might not be the wisest place
to have a quiet drink.

"I think we should get out of here, Skeeve."

I don't know when Kalvin rejoined me, but he was there
hovering at my side again. His words echoed my own
thoughts, but sheer snorkiness made me take the opposite
stance.

"Don't be a snob, Kalvin," I muttered. "Besides, sitting
down for a while was *your* idea, wasn't it?"

Before he could answer, I strode to one of the tables and
plopped down in a seat, raising one hand to signal the
bartender. He ignored it and returned to his conversation
with the other drinkers.

"C'mon, Skeeve. Let's catch a cab back to the hotel and
have our conversation there," Kalvin said, joining me.
"You're in no frame of mind to start drinking. It'll only
make things worse."

He made a lot of sense. Unfortunately, for the mood I
was in, he made too much sense.

"You heard the Butterfly, Kalvin. I've been letting too
many other people run my life by listening to their well-

meaning advice. I'm supposed to start doing what I want to do more often . . . and what I want to do right now is have a drink . . . here."

For a moment I thought he was going to argue with me, but then he gave a sigh and floated down to sit on the table itself.

"Suit yourself," he said. "I suppose everyone's entitled to make a jackass out of themselves once in a while."

"What'll it be?"

The bartender was looming over my table, saving me from having to think of a devastating comeback for Kalvin's jibe. Apparently, now that he had established that he wouldn't come when summoned, he wanted to take my order.

"I'll have . . . "

Suddenly, a glass of wine didn't feel right. Unfortunately, my experience with drinks was almost as limited as my experience with members of the opposite sex.

" . . . Oh, just give me a round of whatever they're drinking at the bar there."

The bartender gave a grunt that was neither approving nor disapproving and left, only to return a few moments later with a small glass of liquid which he slammed down on the table hard enough for some of the contents to slop over the edge. I couldn't see it too clearly, but it seemed to be filled with an amber fluid with bubbles in it that gathered in a froth at the top.

"Ya gotta pay by the round," he sneered, as if it were an insult.

I fished a handful of small change out of my pocket and tossed it on the table, reaching for the glass with the other hand.

Now, some of you might be wondering why I was so willing to experiment with a strange drink after everything

I've been saying about food on Perv. Well, truth to tell, I was sort of hoping this venture would end in disaster. You see, by this time I had cooled off enough to acknowledge that Kalvin was probably right about going back to the hotel, but I had made such a big thing out of making an independent decision that changing my mind now would be awkward. Somewhere in that train of thought, it occurred to me that if this new drink made me sick, I would have an unimpeachable reason for reversing my earlier decision. With that in mind, I raised the glass to my lips and took a sip.

The icy burst that hit my throat was such a surprise that I involuntarily took another swallow . . . and another. I hadn't realized how thirsty I was after my brisk walk until I hit the bottom of the glass without setting it down or taking a breath. Whatever this stuff was, it was absolutely marvelous, and the vaguely bitter aftertaste only served to remind me I wanted more.

"Bring me another of these," I ordered the bartender, who was still sorting through my coins. "And can you bring it in a larger container?"

"I could bring you a pitcher," he grumbled.

"Perfect . . . and pull a little extra there for your trouble."

"Say . . . thanks."

The bartender's mood and opinion of me seemed to have improved as he made his way to the bar. I congratulated myself for remembering what Edvik had said about tipping.

"I suppose it would be pushy to try to point out that you're drinking on an empty stomach," the Djin said drily.

"Not at all," I grinned.

For once I was ahead of him and raised my voice to call the bartender.

"Say! Could you bring me some of that popcorn while you're at it?"

Most of the bar snacks that were laid out seemed to be

in mesh-covered containers to keep them from crawling or hopping away. Amidst these horrors, however, I had spotted a bin of popcorn when I came in, and had made special note of it; thinking that at least some forms of junk food appeared to be the same from dimension to dimension.

"Happy now?"

"I'd be happier if you picked something that was a little less salty," Kalvin grimaced, "but I suppose it's better than nothing."

The bartender delivered my pitcher along with a basket of popcorn, then wandered off to greet some new patrons who had just wandered in. I tossed a handful of the popcorn into my mouth and chewed it while I refilled my glass from the pitcher. It was actually more spicy than salty, which made me revise some of my earlier thoughts about the universality of junk food, but I decided not to mention this discovery to Kalvin. He was fussing at me enough already.

"So, what do you want to talk about?" I said, forcing myself not to immediately wash down the popcorn with a long drink from the glass.

The Djin leaned back and cocked an eyebrow at me.

"Well, your mood seems to have improved, but I was under the impression *you* might want to talk about the Butterfly's advice this afternoon."

As soon as he spoke, my current bubble of levity popped and my earlier depression slammed into me like a fist. Without thinking I drained half the contents of my glass.

"I don't know, Kalvin. I've got a lot of respect for the Butterfly, and I'm sure he meant well, but what he said has raised a lot of questions in my mind . . . questions I've never really asked myself before."

I topped off my glass casually, hoping the Djin wouldn't notice how fast I was drinking the stuff.

"Questions like . . . ?"

"Well, like . . . What are friends . . . really? On the rare occasions the subject comes up, all people seem to talk about is the need to be needed. All of a sudden I'm not sure I know what that means."

Somehow, my glass had gotten empty again. I refilled it as I continued.

"The more I look at it, the more I think that if you *really* need your friends, it's either a sign of weakness or laziness. You either need or want people to do your thinking for you, or your fighting for you, or whatever. Things that by rights you should be able to do for yourself. By rights, that makes you a parasite, existing by leeching off other people's strength and generosity."

I started to take a drink and realized I was empty. I suspected there was a leak in the glass, but set it aside, resolving to let it sit there for a while before I tried refilling it again.

"On the other hand, if you *don't* need your friends, what good are they? Friends take up a big hunk of your time and cause a lot of heartache, so if you don't really need them, why should you bother? In a sense, if they need you, then you're encouraging them into being parasites instead of developing strength on their own. I don't know. What do you think, Kalvin?"

I gestured at him with my glass, and realized it was full again. So much for my resolve. I also realized the pitcher was almost empty.

"That's a rough one, Skeeve," the Djin was saying, and I tried to focus on his words. "I think everybody has to reach their own answer, though it's a rare person who even thinks to ask the question. I will say it's an over-simplification to try to equate caring about someone with weakness, just as I think it's wrong to assume that if we can learn from our friends, they're actually controlling our thinking."

He stopped and stared at my hand. I followed his gaze and realized I was trying to fill my empty glass from an empty pitcher.

"I also think," he sighed, "that we should *definitely* head back to the hotel now. Have you paid the tab? Are we square here?"

"Thass another thing," I said, fighting to get the words out past my tongue, which suddenly seemed to have a mind of its own. "What he said about money. I haven't been using my money right."

"For cryin' out loud, Skeeve! Lower your voice!"

"No, really! I've got all thissh money . . ."

I fumbled my moneybelt out and emptied the gold onto the table.

". . . And has it made ME happy? Has it made ANY-BODY happy?"

When no answer came, I blinked my eyes, trying to get Kalvin back into focus. When he finally spoke, he seemed to be very tense, though his voice was very quiet.

"I think you may have just made someone happy, but I don't think it'll be you."

That's when I noticed the whole bar was silent. Looking around, I was surprised to see how many people had come in while we were talking. It was an ugly-looking crowd, but no one seemed to be talking to each other or doing anything. They just stood there looking at me . . . or to be more exact, looking at the table covered with my money.

Chapter Twelve:

"HOLY BATSHIT, FATMAN! I mean . . ."
—ROBIN

"I . . . THINK I'VE made a tactic . . . tacl . . . an error,"
I whispered with as much dignity as I could muster.

"You can say that again," Kalvin shot back mercilessly.
"You forgot the first rule of survival: Don't tease the animals. Look, Skeeve, do you want to get out of here, or do
you want to get out with your money?"

"Want . . . my money." I wasn't *that* drunk . . . or
maybe I was.

The Djin rolled his eyes in exasperation.

"I was afraid of that. That's going to be a little rougher.
Okay, the first thing you do is get that gold out of sight. I
don't think they'll try anything in here. There are too many
witnesses, which means too many ways to split the loot."

I obediently began to pick up the coins. My hands seemed
to lack the dexterity necessary to lead them back into my
moneybelt, so I settled for shoving them into my pockets
as best I could.

The bar was no longer silent. There was a low murmur going around that sounded ominous even in my condition as various knots of patrons put their heads together. Even without the dark looks they kept shooting in my direction it wasn't hard to guess what the subject of their conversation was.

"The way I see it, if there's going to be trouble, it will hit when we leave. That means the trick is to leave without their knowing it. Order another pitcher."

That's when I realized how much I'd already had to drink. For a moment there, I thought the Djin had said . . .

"You want me to . . ."

" . . . Order another pitcher, but whatever you do, don't drink any of it."

That made even less sense, but I followed his instructions and gestured at the bartender who delivered another pitcher with impressive speed.

I paid him from my pocket.

"I don't get it," I said. "Why should I order a pitcher when you say I shouldn't . . ."

"Shut up and listen," Kalvin hissed. "That was so everybody watching you will think you're planning to stick around for a while. In the meantime, we move."

That made even less sense than having some more to drink.

"But, Kalvin . . . most of them are between us and the door! They'll see me . . ."

"Not out the front door, stupid! You see that little hallway in back? That leads to the restrooms. There's also an exit back there which probably opens into an alley. That's the route we're taking."

"How do you know there's an exit back there?" I said suspiciously.

"Because one of the things I do when I come into a new bar is count the exits," the Djin retorted. "It's a habit I suggest you develop if you're going to keep drinking."

"Don't want any more to drink," I managed, my stomach suddenly rebelling at the thought.

"Good boy. Easy now. Nice and casual. Head for the restrooms."

I took a deep breath in a vain effort to clear my head, then stood up . . . or at least I tried to. Somewhere in the process, my foot got tangled in my chair and I nearly lost my balance. I managed not to fall, but the chair went over on its side noisily, drawing more than a few snickers from the roughnecks at the bar.

"That's all right," Kalvin soothed, his voice seeming to come from a great distance. "Now just head down the hallway."

I seemed to be very tall all of a sudden. Moving very carefully, I drew a bead on the opening to the hallway and headed in. I made it without touching the walls on either side and felt a small surge of confidence. Maybe this scheme of Kalvin's would work after all! As he had said, there was an exit door in the wall just short of the restrooms. Without being told, I changed course and pushed out into the alley, easing the door shut behind me. I was out!

"Oops."

I frowned at the Djin.

"What do you mean, 'Oops!'? Didn't you say I should . . ."

"Nice of you to drop by, mister!"

That last was said by a burly Pervect, one of six actually who were blocking our path down the alley. Apparently our little act hadn't fooled everybody.

"Skeeve, I . . ."

"Never mind, Kalvin. I just figured out for myself what 'Oops' means."

"Of course, you know this here's what you'd call a toll-alley. You got to pay to use it."

That was the same individual talking. If he noticed me talking to Kalvin, which to him would look like talking to thin air, he didn't seem to mind or care.

"That's right," one of his cronies chimed in. "We figure what you got in your pockets ought to just about cover it."

"Quick! Back inside!" Kalvin hissed.

"Way ahead of you," I murmured, feeling behind myself for the door.

I found it . . . sort of. The door was there, but there was no handle on this side. Apparently the bar owners wanted it used for exits only. Terrific.

" . . . The only question is: Are you gonna give it to us quietly, or are we gonna have to take it?"

I've faced lynch mobs, soldiers, and sports fans before, but a half-dozen Pervish plug-uglies was the most frightening force I've ever been confronted with. I decided, all by myself, that this would be an excellent time to delegate a problem.

"C'mon, Kalvin! Do something!"

"Like what? I told you I'm no good in a fight."

"Well, do SOMETHING! You're supposed to be the Djin!"

I guess I knew deep inside that carping at Kalvin wouldn't help matters. To my surprise, however, he responded.

"Oh, all right!" he grimaced. "Maybe this will help."

With that, he made a few passes with his hands and . . .

. . . And I was sober! Stone-cold sober!

I looked at him.

"That's all I can do for you," he shrugged. "From here,

you're on your own. At least now you won't have to fight 'em drunk.''

The thugs were starting to pick up boards and pieces of brick from the alley.

"Time's up!'' their leader declared, starting for me.

I smiled at Kalvin.

"I think your analysis of friendship was only a little short of brilliant,'' I said, "There are a couple of points I'd like to go over, though.''

"NOW?'' the Djin shrieked. "This is hardly the time to . . . Look out!''

The leader of the pack was cocking his arms to take a double-handed swing at me with a piece of lumber he had acquired somewhere along the way. As the wood whistled toward its target, which is to say, my head, I made a circular gesture in the air between us with my hand . . . and the board rebounded as if it had struck an invisible wall!

"Magikal ward,'' I informed the gape-mouthed Djin. "It's like a force field, only different. I *did* mention I was a magician, didn't I!''

The gang stopped dead in their tracks at this display; a few had even retreated a few steps.

"Oh, before I forget, thanks for the sobering-up job, Kalvin. You're right. It does make it a lot easier to focus the mind. Anyway, as I was saying, I've gotten a lot of mileage out of wards. They can be used like I just did, as a shield, or . . .''

I made a few quick adjustments to the spell.

'' . . . You can widen them out into a wall or a bubble. Coming?''

I had expanded the ward and was now starting to push the gang back down the alley ahead of us. It was a minor variant of the trick I used to break up a fight at the Big

Game a while back, so I had reason to have confidence in it. I figured we would just walk out of the alley keeping the thugs at a respectful distance, then hail a cab to get us the heck out of there.

The gang leader had turned and trotted out ahead of the others a few paces.

"Cute. Real cute," he called, turning to face me again. "Hadn't figured you for magik. Well, let's see how you handle *this*, wise guy!"

With that, he pulled what looked like a couple of blackboard erasers from the pocket of his jacket. At first, I thought he was going to try to throw them at me, but instead he clapped them together over his head, showering himself with what appeared to be white chalk dust. It would have been funny . . . if he hadn't looked so grim as he started for me again.

Just to be on the safe side, I doubled up on the ward in front of him . . . and he walked right through it!

"That's what I thought!" he called to his cronies, pausing once he had penetrated my defenses. "Real low level stuff. Go to Class Two or heavier, guys . . . in fact, the heavier the better!"

I should have seen it coming . . . maybe would have if I had more time to think. In a dimension that used both magik and technology, there were bound to be counter-magik spells and weapons available. Unfortunately, it seemed I was about to learn about them first hand!

The other gang members were all reaching into their pockets and producing charms or spray cans. I had a bad feeling that my magikal ward wasn't going to protect me much longer. Apparently Kalvin was of the same opinion.

"Quick, Skeeve! Have you got any other tricks up your sleeve?"

"I've always figured that, in times of crisis, it's best to

play through your strongest suit. Still hoping to avoid any actual violence, I pulled my energy out of the wards and threw it into a new disguise: an over-muscled Pervect easily half again as tall as I really was.

"Do you boys *really* want me to get rough?" I shouted, trying as best as I could to make my voice a threatening bass.

I had thought of making myself look like a policeman, but had discarded the idea. With my luck they probably would have surrendered, and then what would I have done with them? I wanted them to run . . . as far out of my life as possible!

It didn't work.

I had barely gotten the words out when a large chunk of brick ripped through the air just over my head . . . passing through what would have been the chest of the disguised me.

"Disguise spell!" the thrower called. "Go for him like we saw him before!"

To say the least, I figured it was time for the better part of valor. Trying to keep my mind under control, which is harder to do than it sounds with half a dozen bully-boys charging down on you, I slapped on a levitation spell and took to the skies.

. . . At least, I tried to.

I was barely airborne when a vise-like grip closed on my ankle.

"I've got him!"

The grip hurt, which made it difficult to concentrate on my spell. Then, too, it seemed the day had taken a lot more out of me than I had realized. Normally, I can, and have, levitated as many as two people besides myself . . . count that as three since one of them was Massha. In the scramble of the moment, however, I was hard pressed to lift myself and the guy who was holding my ankle. I struggled to get him into the air, then something bounced off my head and . . .

The ground slammed into me at an improbable angle, and for a moment, I saw stars. The pressure seemed to be gone from my ankle, but when I opened my eyes, the leader was standing over me with his trusty board in his hands.

"Nice try, wise guy!" he sneered. "But not good enough. Now give me the . . ."

Suddenly he went sprawling as someone piled into him from behind.

"Quick, Mr. Skeeve! Get up!"

It took me a moment to realize it was the street vendor I had spoken to that morning. He crouched over me, facing down the circling gang.

"Hurry up! I can't hold these guys off by myself!"

I wasn't sure I could get up if I wanted to, but at this point I was willing to abandon any hopes of a non-violent solution to our problems. Propping myself up on one elbow, I reached out with my mind, grabbed a garbage can, and sent it sailing through the gang's formation.

"What the . . ."

"Look out!"

If they wanted physical, I'd give it to them. I mentally grabbed two more trash cans and sent them into the fray, keeping all three flying back and forth in the narrow confines of the alley.

"Cripes! I'm on your side! Remember?" the street vendor cried, ducking under one of my missiles.

I summoned up a little more energy and threw a ward over the two of us. Somehow, I didn't think anyone had thought to use their anti-magik stuff on a garbage can.

A few more swings with the old trash cans, and it was all over.

Heaving a ragged breath, I dropped the ward and brought my makeshift weapons to a halt. Four of my attackers lay sprawled on the ground, and the other two had apparently taken to their heels.

"Nice work, Skeeve," Kalvin crowed, appearing from wherever it was he had taken cover when the fracas started.

"Are you all right, Mr. Skeeve?" the street vendor asked, extending a hand to help me to my feet.

"I think so . . . yes . . . thanks to you . . . J.R., isn't it?"

"That's right. I was walkin' home when I saw these jokers pilin' into you. It looked a little uneven, so I thought I'd lend a hand. Cheez! I didn't know you wuz a magician!"

"A mighty grateful magician right now," I said, digging into my pocket. "Here, take this. Consider it my way of saying thank you."

"Excuse me," the Djin drawled, "but didn't we just get into this whole brawl so you could *keep* your money?"

He needn't have worried. J.R. recoiled from the gold as if I had offered him poison.

"I didn't help you for money!" he said through tight lips. "I know you don't mean . . . Cripes! All you rich guys are the same. You think your money . . . Look! I work for my money, see! I ain't no bum lookin' for a handout!"

With that he spun on his heel and marched away, leaving me with an outstretched hand full of gold.

It would have been a beautiful exit, if the alley hadn't suddenly been blocked by a vehicle pulling in . . . a vehicle with blue and red flashing lights on top.

Chapter Thirteen:

"Who? Me, Officer?"

—J. DILLINGER

"I STILL DON'T see why we should be detained."

It seemed like hours that we had been at the police station, we being myself, J.R., and, of course, Kalvin, though the police seemed unaware of the latter's existence and I, in turn, was disinclined to tell them. Despite our protests, we had been transported here shortly after the police had arrived. The thugs had been revived and placed in a separate vehicle, though I noticed they were handled far less gently than we were. Still, it was small consolation to being held against our will.

"You don't? Well, then we'll have to go over it all again slowly and see if you can get a hint."

This was spoken by the individual who had been conducting our interrogation since we arrived. From the deferential way the other policemen treated him, I assumed he was a ranking officer of some sort. He possessed bad breath, a foul disposition, and what seemed to be an endless tolerance for repetition. As he launched into his oration, I fought an impulse to chant along with the now-familiar words.

"We could charge you with Being Drunk in Public."

"I'm stone cold sober," I interrupted, thanking my lucky stars for Kalvin's assistance. "If you don't believe it, test me."

"There are a lot of witnesses who said you were falling down drunk in the bar."

"I tripped over a chair."

"Then there's the minor matter of Assault . . ."

"I keep telling you, they attacked me! It was self-defense!"

". . . And Destruction of Private Property . . ."

"For cryin' out loud, it was a garbage can! I'll pay for a new one if that's . . ."

" . . . And, of course, there's Resisting Arrest."

"I asked them where we were going. That's all."

"That's not the way the arresting officers tell it."

Realizing I was getting nowhere in this argument, I did the next most logical thing: I took out my frustration on an innocent bystander. In this case, the nearest available target happened to be J.R., who seemed to be dozing off in his chair.

"Aren't you going to say anything?" I demanded. "You're in this too, you know."

"There's no need," the street vendor shrugged. "It's not like we were in trouble or anything."

"That's funny. I thought we were in a police station."

"So what? They aren't really serious. Are you, Captain?"

The Pervect who had been arguing with me shot him a dark look, but I noticed he didn't contradict what had been said.

"I'll bite J.R.," I said, still watching the captain. "What are you seeing that I'm not in this situation?"

"It's what *isn't* happening that's the tip-off," he winked. "What isn't happening is we aren't being booked. We've been here a long time and they haven't charged us with any crimes."

"But the Captain here said . . ."

"He said they *could* charge us with etc., etc. You notice he hasn't actually done it. Believe me, Mr. Skeeve, if they were going to jail us, we'd have been behind bars an hour ago. They're just playing games to stall for a while."

What he said seemed incredible considering the amount of grief we were being put through, yet I couldn't find a hole in his logic. I turned to the captain and raised an eyebrow.

"Is that true?" I said.

The policeman ignored me, leaning back in his chair to stare at J.R. through half-closed eyes.

"You seem to know a lot about police procedure, son. Almost as if you've been rousted before."

A sneer spread across the street vendor's face as he met the challenge head on.

"Anyone who works the streets gets hassled," he said. "It's how you police protect the upstanding citizens from merchants like me who are too poor to afford a storefront. I suppose it *is* a lot safer than taking on the real criminals who might shoot back. We should be grateful to our defenders of the law. If it wasn't for them, the dimension would probably be overrun with street vendors and parking violators."

I should have been grateful for the diversion after being on the hot seat myself for so long. Unfortunately, I had also logged in a fair amount of time as the Great Skeeve, and as such was much more accustomed to being hassled than I was to being overlooked.

"I believe the question was 'Are we or are we not being

charged with any crimes?' '' I said pointedly. ''I'm still waiting for an answer.''

The captain glowered at me for a few moments, but when I didn't drop my return gaze, he heaved a sigh.

''No. We won't be bringing any charges against you at this time.''

''Then we're free to go?''

''Well, there are a few more questions you'll have to answer first. After that, you're free to . . .''

''That's 'more' as in new questions, not the same ones all over again. Right?''

The policeman glared at me, but now that I knew we were in the clear, I was starting to have fun with this.

''That's right,'' he said through gritted teeth.

''Okay. Shoot.''

I suddenly realized that was an unfortunate use of words in a room full of armed policemen, but it escaped unnoticed.

The captain cleared his throat noisily before continuing.

''Mister Skeeve,'' he began formally, ''do you wish to press charges against the alleged attackers we currently have in custody?''

''What kind of a silly question is that? Of course I want to.''

Kalvin was waving frantically at me and pointing to J.R. The street vendor was shaking his head in a slow, but firm, negative.

'' . . . Um . . . before I make up my mind on that, Captain,'' I hedged, trying to figure out what J.R. was thinking, ''could you tell me what happens if I don't press charges?''

''We can probably hold onto them until tomorrow morning for questioning, but then we'll let them go.''

That didn't sound like particularly satisfying treatment for a gang that had tried to rob me. Still, J.R. seemed to know what he was doing so far, and I was disinclined to go against his signaled advice.

" . . . And if I DO press charges?" I pressed, trying to sort it out.

"I'm not a judge," the captain shrugged, "so I can't say for sure . . . but I can give you my best guess."

"Please."

"We'll charge them with Attempted Robbery and Assault with Intent To Do Great Bodily Harm . . . I don't think we could make Attempted Murder stick."

That sounded pretty good to me, but the policeman wasn't finished.

" . . . Then the court will appoint a lawyer—if they don't already have one—who will arrange for bail to be set. They'll probably raise the money from a bondsman and be back on the streets before noon tomorrow."

"What? But they . . ."

"It'll take a couple of months for the trial to be scheduled, at which point it'll be your word against theirs . . . and they're not only locals, they have you outnumbered."

I was starting to see the light.

" . . . That is, if it gets to trial. More than likely there'll be some plea bargaining, and they'll plead guilty to a lesser charge, which means a smaller sentence with an earlier parole—if the sentence isn't suspended as soon as it's handed down . . ."

"Whoa! Stop! I think I'll just pass on pressing charges."

"Thought you would," the captain nodded. "It's probably the easiest way for everybody. After all, you weren't hurt, and you've still got your money."

"Of course, the next person they jump may not be quite so lucky" I said drily.

"I didn't say it was the best way to handle it, just the easiest."

Before I could think of a witty answer to that one, a uniformed policeman rapped at the doorframe, entered the room, and passed a sheet of paper to the captain. Something about the way the latter's lips tightened as he scanned the sheet made me nervous.

"Well, well, *Mis*-ter Skeeve," he said at last, dropping the paper onto the desk in front of him. "It seems this isn't the first time you've dealt with the police since arriving in this dimension."

"Uh-oh," Kalvin exclaimed, rolling his eyes, "here it comes!"

"What makes you say that, Captain?"

I had a hunch it wouldn't do any good to act innocent. Unfortunately, I didn't have any other ideas about how to act.

"What makes me say that is the report I just received. I thought I should check with the other precincts to see if they had heard of you, and it seems they have."

"*That's* why they've been stalling," J.R. put in. "To wait until the reports came in. It's called police efficiency."

The captain ignored him.

"According to this, you've had two run-ins with the police already. First for acting suspicious on the public streets . . ."

"I was being polite instead of barreling into people!" I broke in, exasperated. "I'm sorry, I was new here and didn't know 'rude' was the operative word for this dimension. You should put up signs or something warning people that being polite is grounds for harassment on Perv!"

The captain continued as if I hadn't spoken.

" . . . And later that same day, you tried to get out of paying for a pretty expensive meal."

"I fainted, for Pete's sake! As soon as I came to, I paid for the meal, even though I hadn't eaten a bite."

"Now that in itself sounds a little suspicious," the captain said, pursing his lips. "Why would you order a meal you couldn't, or wouldn't, eat?"

"Because I didn't know I couldn't eat it when I ordered it, obviously. I keep telling you . . . I'm new here!"

"Uh huh," the policeman leaned back and studied me through slitted eyes. "You've got a glib answer for everything . . . don't you, Mister Skeeve."

"That's because it's true! Would I be less suspicious if I *didn't* have answers for your questions? Tell me, Captain, I really want to know! I know I'm not a criminal, what does it take to convince *you?*"

The captain shook his head slowly.

"Frankly, I don't know. I've been on the force for a long time, and I've learned to trust my instincts. Your story *sounds* good, but my instinct tells me you're trouble looking for a place to happen."

I could see I was playing into a stacked deck, so I abandoned the idea of impressing him with my innocence.

"I guess the bottom line is the same as before that sheet came in, then. Are you going to press charges against me . . . or am I free to go?"

He studied me for a few more moments, then waved his hand.

"Go on. Get out of here . . . and take your little street buddy with you. Just take my advice and don't carry so much cash in the future. There's no profit in teasing the animals."

If I had been thinking, I would have let it go at that. Unfortunately, it had been a long day and I was both tired and annoyed . . . a dangerous combination.

"I'll remember that, Captain," I said, rising to my feet. "I had been under the impression that the police were around to protect innocent citizens like me . . . not to waste everybody's time harassing them. Believe me, I've learned my lesson.''

Every policeman in the room suddenly tensed, and I realized too late that there was also no profit in critiquing the police.

'' . . . And if we don't check on suspicious characters *before* they make trouble, then all we're good for is filling out reports AFTER a crime had been committed,'' the captain spat bitterly. ''Either way, 'innocent citizens' like you can find something to gripe about!''

''I'm sorry, Captain. I shouldn't have . . .''

I don't know if he even heard my attempted apology. If he did, it didn't make a difference.

''You see, I've learned my lesson, too. When I first joined the force, I thought there was nothing better I could do with my life than to spend it protecting innocent citizens . . . and I still believe that. Even then I knew this would be a thankless occupation. What I *hadn't* realized was that 'innocent citizens' like you are not only ungrateful, the tendency is to treat the police like they're enemies!''

I decided against trying to interrupt him. He was on a roll, lecturing about what seemed to be his favorite subject. Opening my mouth now would probably be about as safe as getting between my pet dragon, Gleep, and his food dish.

''Everybody wants the crooks to be in jail, but nobody wants a prison in their community . . . or to vote in the taxes to build new jails. So the prisons we have are over-crowded, and the 'innocent citizens' scream bloody murder every time a judge suspends a sentence or lets an offender out on parole.''

He was up and pacing back and forth now as he warmed to his subject.

''Nobody sees the crimes that aren't committed. We can reduce the crime rate 98%, and the 'innocent citizens' blame

US for that last 2% . . . as if we were the ones committing the crimes! Nobody wants to cooperate with the police or approve the tax allocations necessary to keep up with inflation, so we can't even keep abreast of where we are, much less expand to keep up with the population growth.''

He paused and leveled an accusing finger at J.R.

''Then there are 'innocent citizens' like your buddy here, who admits he's running an illegal, unlicensed business. What that means, incidentally, is that he doesn't have to pay *any* taxes, even the existing ones, although he expects the same protection from us as the storekeepers who *do*, even though most of them cheat on their taxes as well.''

''So we're supposed to keep the peace and apprehend criminals while we're understaffed and using equipment that's outdated and falling apart. About all we *have* to work with is our instincts . . . and then we get hassled for using that!''

He came to a halt in front of me, and pushed his face close to mine, treating me to another blast of his breath. I didn't point it out to him.

''Well *this* time we're going to see just how good my instincts are. I'm letting you go for now, but it occurs to me it might be a good idea to run a check on you on other dimensions. If you're just an innocent businessman like you claim, we won't find anything . . . but if I'm right,'' he gave me a toothy grin, ''you've probably tangled with the law before, and we'll find that too. I'm betting you've left a trail of trouble behind you, a trail that leads right to here. If so, we'll be talking again . . . real soon. I don't want you to switch hotels or try to leave the dimension without letting me know, understand? I want to be able to find you again, MISTER Skeeve!''

Chapter Fourteen:

"Parting is such sweet sorrow."

—FIGARO

THE POSSIBILITY OF an extensive check on my off-dimension background worried me, but not so much that I forgot
my manners. J.R. had saved my skin in the alley fight,
and, throughout the police grilling, a part of my mind had
been searching for a way to repay him. As we left the police
station, I thought I had the answer.

"Say, J.R.," I said, turning to him on the steps, "about
that business you want to start . . . how much capital would
you need to get started?"

I could see his neck stiffening as I spoke.

"I told you before, Mr. Skeeve, I won't take a reward
for saving your life."

"Who said anything about a reward? I'm talking about
investing in your operation and taking a share of the profits."

That one stopped him in his tracks.

"You'd do that?"

"Why not? I'm a businessman and always try to keep an
eye open for new ventures to back. The trickiest thing is

finding trustworthy principals to manage the investments. In your case, you've already proved to me that you're trustworthy. So how much would you need for this plan of yours?''

The street vendor thought for a few moments.

"Even *with* backing I'd want to start small and build. Figuring that . . . yeah. I think about five thousand in gold would start things off right.''

"Oh,'' I said, intelligently. I wasn't about to question his figures, but the start-up cost was higher than I had expected. I only had a couple thousand with me, and most of that was going to cover Edvick's services and the hotel bill. So much for a grand gesture!

"I'll . . . uh . . . have to think about it.''

J.R.'s face fell.

"Yeah. Sure. Well, you know where to find me when you make up your mind.''

He turned and strode off down the street without looking back. It was silly to feel bad about not fulfilling an offer I didn't have to make, but I did.

"Well, I guess it's time for us to head back to the hotel . . . right Skeeve?'' Kalvin chimed in.

I had botched the job with J. R., but I resolved that this one I was going to do right.

"No,'' I said.

"No?'' the Djin echoed. "So where are we going instead?''

"That's the whole point, Kalvin. *We* aren't going anywhere. *I'm* going back to the hotel. *You're* going back to Djinger.''

He floated up to eye level with me, frowning as he cocked his head to one side.

"I don't get it. Why should I go back to Djinger?''

"Because you've filled your contract. That means you're

free to go, so I assume you're going.''

''I did?''

''Sure. Back in the alley. You used a spell to sober me up before I had to fight those goons. To my thinking, that fulfills your contract.''

The Djin stroked his beard thoughtfully.

''I dunno,'' he said. ''That wasn't much of a spell.''

''You never promised much,'' I insisted. ''As a matter of fact, you went to great lengths to impress me with how little you could do.''

''Oh, that,'' Kalvin waved his hand deprecatingly. ''That's just the standard line of banter we feed to the customers. It keeps them from expecting too much of a Djin. You'd be amazed at some of the things folks expect us to do. If we can keep their expectations low, then they're easier to impress when we strut our stuff.''

''Well it worked. I'm impressed. If you hadn't done your thing back there in the alley, my goose would have been cooked before J.R. hit the scene.''

''Glad to help. It was less dangerous than trying to lend a hand in the fight.''

''Maybe, but by my count it still squares things between us. You promised one round of minor help, and delivered it at a key moment. That's all your contract called for . . . and more.''

The Djin folded his arms and stared, frowning into the distance for several moments.

''Check me on this, Skeeve,'' he said finally, ''I've been helpful to you so far, right?''

''Right,'' I nodded, wondering what he was leading up to.

''And I've been pretty good company, haven't I? I mean, I do tend to run off at the mouth a bit, but overall you haven't seemed to mind having me around.''

''Right again.''

"So why are you trying to get rid of me?"

Suddenly, the whole day caught up with me. The well meant advice from the Butterfly, the drinking, the fight, the head-butting with the police all swelled within me until my mind and temper burst from the pressure.

"I'M NOT TRYING TO GET RID OF YOU!!" I shrieked at the Djin, barely aware my voice had changed. "Don't you think I want to keep you around? Don't you think I know that my odds of finding Aahz on my own in this wacko dimension are next to zip? Dammit, Kalvin, I'M TRYING TO BE NICE TO YOU!!!"

"Um . . . maybe you could be a little less nice and quit shouting?"

I realized that I had backed him across the sidewalk and currently had him pinned against the wall with the force of my "niceness." I took a long, deep breath and tried to bring myself under control.

"Look," I said carefully, "I didn't mean to yell at you. It's just . . ."

Something trickled down my face and it dawned on me that I was on the verge of tears. On the verge, heck! I was starting to cry. I cleared my throat noisily, covertly wiping away the tear as I covered my mouth, hoping Kalvin wouldn't notice. If he did, he was too polite to say anything.

"Let me try this again from the top."

I drew a ragged breath.

"You've been a big help, Kalvin, more than I could have ever hoped for when I opened your vial. Your advice has been solid, and if I've been having trouble it's because I didn't listen to it enough."

I paused, trying to organize my thoughts.

"I'm not trying to get rid of you . . . really. I'd like nothing better than to have you stick around at least until I found Aahz. I just don't want to trade on our friendship. I got your services in a straightforward business deal . . . one you had no say in, if your account of how Djinger works is accurate. If I sounded a bit cold when I told you I thought our contract was complete, it's because I was fighting against begging you to stay. I was afraid that if I did, it would put you in a bad position . . . actually, it would put *me* in a bad position. If I made a big appeal to you and you said no, it would leave us both feeling pretty bad at the end of what otherwise has been a mutually beneficial association. The only thing I could think of that would be worse would be if you agreed to stay out of pity. Then I'd feel guilty as long as you were around, knowing all the while that you could and should be going about your own business, and would be if I weren't so weak that I can't handle a simple task by myself.''

The tears were running freely now, but I didn't bother trying to hide them. I just didn't care anymore.

''Mostly what you've done,'' I continued, ''is to keep me company. I've felt scared and alone ever since I hit this dimension . . . or would have if you hadn't been along. I'm so screaming afraid of making a mistake that I'd probably freeze up and do nothing unless I had somebody in tow to applaud when I did right and to carp at me when I did wrong . . . just so I'd know the difference. That's how insecure I am . . . I don't even trust my own judgment as to whether I'm right or not in what I do! The trouble is, I haven't been doing so well in the friendship department lately. Aahz walked out on me, the M.Y.T.H. team thinks I've deserted them . . . heck, I even managed to offend J.R. by trying to say thanks with my wallet instead of my mouth.''

It occurred to me I was starting to ramble. Making a feeble pass at my tear-streaked face with my sleeve, I forced a smile.

"Anyway, I can't see imposing on you, either as a friend or a business associate, just to hold my hand in troubled times. That doesn't mean I'm not grateful for what you've done or that I'm trying to get rid of you. I'd appreciate it if you stuck around but I don't think I have any right to ask you to."

Having run out of things to say, I finished with a half-hearted shrug. Strangely enough, after bearing my soul and clearing my mind of the things which had been troubling me, I felt worlds better.

"Are you through?"

Kalvin was still hovering patiently with his arms folded. Perhaps it was my imagination, but there seemed to be a terse edge to his voice.

"I guess so. Sorry for running on like that."

"No problem. Just as long as I get my innings."

"Innings?"

"A figure of speech," he waved. "In this case, it means it's my turn to talk and your turn to listen. I've tried before, but it seems like every time I start, we get interrupted . . . or you get drunk."

I grimaced at the memory.

"I didn't mean to get drunk. It's just that I've never . . ."

"Hey! Remember? It's my turn," the Djin broke in. "I want to say . . . just a second."

He made a sweeping gesture with his hand and . . . grew! Suddenly he was the same size I was.

"There, that's better!" he said, dusting his hands together. "It'll be a littler harder to overlook me now."

I was about to ask for a full accounting of his "meager" powers, but his last comment had stung me.

"I'm sorry, Kalvin. I didn't mean to . . ."

"Save it!" he ordered, waving his hand. "Right now it's my turn. There'll be lots of time later for you to wallow in guilt. If not, I'm sure you'll make the time.''

That had a nasty sound to it, but I subsided and gestured for him to continue.

"Okay," he said, "first, last, and in between, you're wrong, Skeeve. It's hard for me to believe such a right guy can be so wrong."

It occurred to me that I had already admitted my confidence in my perception of right and wrong was at an all time low. I didn't verbalize it, though. Kalvin had said he wanted a chance to have his say, and I was going to do my best to not interrupt. I owed him that much.

"Ever since we met, you've been talking about right and wrong as if they were absolutes. According to you, things are either right or they're wrong . . . period. 'Was Aahz right to leave?' . . . Are you wrong to try to bring him back? . . . Well, my young friend, life isn't that simple. Not only are you old enough to know that, you'd better learn it before you drive yourself and everyone around you absolutely crazy!"

He began to float back and forth in the air in front of me with his hands clasped behind his back. I supposed it was his equivalent of pacing.

"It's possible for you, or anyone else to not be right and still not be wrong, just as you can be right from a business standpoint, but wrong from a humanitarian viewpoint. The worlds are complex, and people are a hopeless tangle of contradictions. Conditions change not only from situation to situation and person to person, but from moment to moment as well. Trying to kid yourself that there's some master key to what's right and wrong is ridiculous . . . worse than that, it's dangerous, because you'll always end up feeling incompetent and inadequate when it eludes you."

Even though I was having trouble grasping what he was saying, that last part rang a bell. It described with uncomfortable accuracy how I felt about myself more often than not! I tried to listen more closely.

"You've got to accept that life is complicated and often frustrating. What's right for you may not be right for Aahz. There are even times when there is no right answer . . . just the least objectionable of several bad choices. Recognize that, then don't waste time and energy wondering why it is or railing that it's unfair . . . accept it."

"I . . . I'll try," I said "but it's not easy."

"Of course it's not easy!" the Djin shot back. "Who ever said it was easy? Nothing's easy. Sometimes it's less difficult than at other times, but it's never easy. Part of your problem is that you keep thinking things should be easy, so you assume the easy way is the right way. Case in point: You knew it would be hard to ask me to stay on after I had fulfilled the contract, so you decided the right thing to do was not to ask . . . ignoring how hard it would be for you to keep hunting for Aahz without me."

"But if it would be easier for me if you stayed . . ."

"That's right. It's a contradiction," Kalvin grinned. "Confusing, isn't it? Forget right and wrong for a while. What do *you* want?"

That one *was* easy.

"I'd like you to stay and help me look for Aahz," I said firmly.

The Djin smiled and nodded.

"Not a chance," he replied.

"What?"

"Did I stutter? I said . . ."

"I know what you said!" I cut him off. "It's just that you said . . . I mean before you said . . ."

"Oh, there's no problem in your asking me . . . or in your terms. I'm just not going to stay."

By now my head was spinning with confusion, but I tried

to maintain what little poise I had left.

" . . . But I thought . . . Oh, well. I guess I was mistaken."

"No you weren't. If you had asked me in the first place, I would have stayed."

"Then why . . ." I began, but the Djin waved me into silence.

"I'm sorry, Skeeve. I shouldn't tease you with head games at a time like this. What changed my mind was something you said while you were explaining why you didn't ask. You said you were scared and insecure, which is only sane, all things considered. But then you added something about how you were afraid to trust your own judgment and therefore needed someone else along to tell you whether you were right or not."

He paused and shook his head.

"I can't go along with that. I realized then that if I stayed, I'd fall into the same trap all your other colleagues have . . . of inadvertently doing your thinking for you when we express our own opinions. The sad thing is that we aren't, really. You decide yourself what advice you do and don't listen to. The trouble is, you only remember when you go against advice and it goes wrong . . . like when you got drunk tonight. Any correct judgment calls you assume were made by your 'advisors.' Well, you've convinced me that you're a right guy, Skeeve. Now all you have to do is convince yourself. That's why I'm going to head on back to Djinger and let you work this problem out on your own. Right or wrong, there'll be no one to take the credit or share the blame. It's all yours. I'm betting your solution will be right."

He held out his hand. I took it and carefully shook hands with this person who had been so much help to me.

"I . . . well, thanks, Kalvin. You've given me a lot to think about."

"It's been a real pleasure, Skeeve . . . really. Good luck in finding our friend. Oh, say . . ."

He dug something out of his waistband and placed it in my hand. As he released it, it grew into a full-sized business card.

"That's my address on Djinger. Stay in touch . . . even if it's just to let me know how this whole thing turns out."

"I will," I promised. "Take care of yourself, Kalvin . . . and thanks again!"

"Oh, and one more thing . . . about your having problems with your friends? Forget trying to be strong. Your real strength is in being a warm, caring person. When you *try* to be strong, it comes across as being cold and insensitive. Think about it."

He gave one last wave, folded his arms, and faded from view.

I stared at the empty space for a few moments, then started the walk back to my hotel alone. I knew where it was . . . what I *didn't* know was where Djinger was.

Chapter Fifteen:

"Easy credit terms available . . ."

—SATAN

"I HEAR YOU got jumped last night."

I paused in mid-move of easing myself into the cab's back seat to give the cabbie a long stare.

" . . . And good morning to you, too, Edvick," I said drily. "Yes, thank you, I slept very well."

My sarcasm was not lost on the driver . . . a fact for which I was secretly grateful. Sometimes I have cause to wonder about my powers of communication.

"Hey! Nothing personal. It's just that people talk, ya know?"

"No, I don't . . . but I'm learning."

It seemed that however large and populated Perv appeared to be, there was a thriving network of gossip lurking just out of sight.

I had come down early, hoping to have a chance to talk with J.R., but between my room and the front door I had been stopped by two bellhops and the desk clerk, all of whom knew that I had been in a fight the night before. Of

course, they each expressed their sympathies . . . in varying
degrees. As I recall, the desk clerk's sympathy went something like "You're welcome to use the hotel safe for your
valuables, sir . . . but we can't accept responsibility for any
losses."

Terrific!!

I had rapidly discovered that I wasn't wild about the idea
of my escapade being discussed by the general populace.
Especially not since it ended with a session with the police.

Even though he had noted my displeasure at discussing
the prior night's incident, Edvick seemed determined not to
let the subject die as we started on our way.

"I told you you should have gotten a bodyguard," he
lectured. "Carrying that kind of cash around is just askin'
for trouble."

"Funny, the police said the same thing . . . about the
cash, I mean."

"Well they're right . . . for a change. Things are dangerous enough around here without drawing unnecessary attention to yourself."

I leaned back in the seat and closed my eyes. I hadn't
slept well, but the brief time I had spent in a horizontal
position had allowed my muscles to tighten, and I ached all
over.

"So, I discovered," I said. "Oh well, it's over now.
Besides, I didn't do such a bad job of taking care of myself."

"The way I heard it, someone showed up to help bail
you out," Edvick pointed out bluntly, "and even then it
was touch and go. Don't kid yourself about it being over,
though. You'd just better hope your luck holds the next
time."

Suddenly, my aching muscles were no longer the main
claim to my attention.

"Next time?" I said, sitting up straight. "What next time?"

"I don't want to sound pessimistic," the cabbie shrugged, "but I figure it's a given. Those guys you messed up are going to be back on the street today, and will probably devote a certain amount of their time and energy trying to find you for a rematch."

"You think so?"

"Then again, even if I'm wrong, the word is out that you're carrying a good sized wad around with you. That's going to make you fair game for every cheap hoodlum looking to pick up some quick cash."

I hadn't stopped to consider it, but what Edvick was saying made sense. All I needed to make my mission more difficult was to have to be watching my back constantly at the same time!

"I'm sorry, what was that again?" I said, trying to concentrate on what the driver was saying.

"Huh? Oh, I was just sayin' again that what you should really do is hire a bodyguard . . . same as I've been sayin' right along."

He *had* been saying that all along, and Kalvin had agreed with him. I had poo-pooed the idea originally, but now I was forced to reexamine my stance on the matter.

"Nnnnno," I said, finally, talking to myself. "I can't do it."

"Why not?" Edvick chimed in, adding his two cents to the argument drawing to a close in my mind.

"Well, the most overpowering reason is that I can't afford one."

The cabbie snorted.

"You've got to be kidding me. With the money you've got?"

"It may seem like a lot, but nearly all of it is already committed to you and the hotel."

The cab swerved dangerously as Edvick turned in his seat to stare at me.

"You mean that's all the money you have? You're carrying your whole bankroll?"

As upset as I was, that thought made me laugh.

"Not hardly," I said. "The trouble is that most of my money is back on Deva. I only brought some of it along for pocket expenses. Unfortunately I badly underestimated what the prices would be like here, so I have to keep an eye on my expenses."

"Oh, that's no problem," the cabbie retorted, turning his attention to the road again. "Just open a line of credit here."

"Do what?"

"Talk to a bank and borrow what you need against your assets. That's how I came up with the money for this cab . . . not to mention my other ventures. Sheese! If everybody tried to operate on a cash basis, it would ruin the dimension's economy!"

"I don't know," I hesitated. "Nobody on this dimension really knows me. Do you really think a bank would be willing to trust me with a loan?"

"There's only one way to find out," Edvick shrugged. "Tell you what . . . there's a branch of my bank not far from here. Why don't you pop in and talk to them. You might be surprised."

The bank itself was not particularly imposing; a medium-sized storefront with a row of teller windows and a few scattered desks. Some doors in the back wall presumably led to offices and the vault, but they were painted assorted bright colors and in themselves did not appear particularly ominous. Still, I realized I felt no small degree of nervousness as I surveyed the interior. There were small clues here and there which bespoke a seriousness which belied the studied casualness of the decor. Little things, like the machines mounted high in the corners which constantly swept the room as if monitoring the movements of both tellers and customers. The tellers themselves were secure behind high panes of innocent-looking glass, doing business through an ingenious slot and drawer arrangement at each station. An observant person such as myself, however, could not help but notice that if the degree of distortion were any indication, the glass was much thicker than it might first appear. There were also armed guards scattered around the room draped with an array of weapons which did not look at all ceremonial or decorative. There was a great deal of money here, and an equally great effort was being made to be sure no one decided to simply help themselves to the surplus.

I had a hunch the kind of business I had in mind would not be handled over the counter by a teller, and, sure enough when I inquired, I was ushered immediately through one of the brightly painted doors into a private office.

The individual facing me across the desk rose and extended a hand in greeting as I entered. He was impeccably dressed in a business suit of what could only be called a conservative cut . . . particularly for a Pervect, and he oozed a sincere warmth that bordered on oily. Green scales and yellow eyes notwithstanding, he reminded me of Grimble, the Chancellor of the Exchequer I had feuded with back at Possiltum. I wondered briefly if this was common with professional money guardians, everywhere . . . maybe it was something in a ledger paper. If so, it boded ill for my dealing today . . . Grimble and I never really got along.

"Come in, come in," the individual purred. "Please, have a seat Mister . . . ?"

"Skeeve," I said, sinking into the indicated chair. "And it's just 'Skeeve,' not Mr. Skeeve."

I had never been wild about the formality of "Mister" title, and after having it hissed at me by the police the night before, I was developing a positive aversion to it.

"Of course, of course," he nodded, reseating himself. "My name is Malcolm."

Perhaps it was his similarity to Grimble, but I was finding his habit of repeating himself to be a growing annoyance. I reminded myself that I was trying to court his favor and made an effort to shake the feeling off.

" . . . And how can we be of service to you today?"

"Well, Malcolm, I'm a businessman visiting here on Perv," I said, aware as I spoke that I was unconciously falling into a formal speech pattern. "My expenses have been running a bit higher than I anticipated, and frankly my ready cash supply is lower than I find comfortable. Someone suggested that I might open a line of credit with your bank, so I stopped in to see if there was any possibility we might work something out."

"I see."

He ran his eyes over me, and much of the warmth went out of the room. I was suddenly acutely aware of how I was dressed.

After overdressing for my interview with the Butterfly, I had decided to stick with my normal, comfortable, informal appearance. I had anticipated that bankers would be more conservative than financiers, and that a bank would probably be equipped to detect disguise spells, so it would be wisest if I was as open and honest as possible. Courtesy of a crash course by Bunny, my administrative assistant, on how to dress, my wardrobe was nothing to be embarrassed about, but I probably didn't look like most of the businessmen Malcolm was used to dealing with. His visual assessment

of me reminded me of the once-over I would get when
encountering a policeman . . . only more so. I had a feeling
the banker could tell me how much money I had in my
pockets down to the loose change.

"What line of work did you say you were in, Mister
Skeeve?"

I noted that the "Mister" had reappeared, but wasn't up
to arguing over it.

"I'm a magician . . . Well, actually I'm the president of
an association of magicians . . . a corporation."

I managed to stop there before I started babbling. I've
noticed a tendency in myself to run on when I'm nervous.

" . . . And the name of your corporation?"

"Um . . . M.Y.T.H. Inc."

He jotted the information down on a small notepad.

"Your home offices are on Klah?"

"No. We operate out of Deva . . . At the Bazaar."

He glanced up at me with his eyebrows raised, then caught
himself and regained his composure.

"Would you happen to know what bank you deal with
on Deva?"

"Bank? I mean, not really. Aahz and Bunny . . . our
financial section usually handles that end of the business."

Any hope I had of a credit line went out the window. I
didn't know for sure we *did* any banking. Aahz was a stickler
for keeping our funds readily available. I couldn't imagine
a bank wanting to deal with someone who didn't trust banks,
or to take my word for what our cash holdings were . . .
even if I *knew* what they were.

The banker was studying his notes.

"Of course you understand, we'll have to run a check
on this."

I started to rise. At this point all I wanted was out of his
office.

"Certainly," I said, trying to maintain a modicum of poise. "How long will that take, just so I'll know when to contact you again?"

Malcolm waved a casual hand at me as he turned to a keyboard at the side of his desk.

"Oh, it won't take any time at all. I'll just use the computer to take a quick peek. I should have an answer in a couple of seconds."

I couldn't make up my mind whether to be astonished or concerned. Astonished won out.

" . . . But my office is on Deva," I said, repeating myself unnecessarily.

"Quite right," the banker responded absently as he hammered busily on the keys. "Fortunately, computers and cats can see and work right through dimensional barriers. The trick is to get them to do it when you want them to instead of when they feel like it."

Of the assorted thoughts which whirled in my mind at this news, only one stood out.

"Do the police have computers?"

"Not of this quality or capacity." He favored me with a smug, tight-lipped smile. "Civil services don't have access to the same financial resources that banks do . . . Ah! Here we go."

He leaned forward and squinted at the computer's screen, which I couldn't see from where I sat. I wondered if it was coincidence that the view was blocked from the visitor's chair, then decided it was a silly question.

"Impressive. Very impressive indeed." He shot a glance at me. "Might I ask who handles your portfolio?"

"My portfolio? I'm not an artist. I'm a magician . . . like I told you."

"An artist. That's a good one, Skeeve . . . you don't mind if I call you Skeeve, do you?" The banker laughed as if we shared a mutual joke. "I meant your portfolio of stocks and investments."

His original warmth had returned . . . and then some. Whatever he had seen on the screen had definitely improved his opinion of me.

"Oh. That would be Bunny. She's my administrative assistant."

"I hope you pay her well. Otherwise some other outfit might be tempted to swoop down and hire her away from you."

From his tone, I could make a pretty good guess as to which outfit might be interested in doing just that.

"Among other things, she holds stock in our operation." I said pointedly.

"Of course, of course. Just a thought. Well Mis . . . Skeeve, I'm sure we can provide you with adequate financial support during your stay on Perv. What's more I hope you'll keep us in mind should you ever want to open an office here and need to open a local account."

Pervects have an exceptional number of teeth, and Malcolm seemed determined to show all of his to me without missing a syllable. I was starting to get impressed myself. I had known our operation was doing well, but had never stopped to assess exactly how well. If the banker's reaction was an accurate gauge, however, we must have been doing very well indeed!

"If you'll give me just a moment here, Skeeve," he said, lunging out of his seat and heading for the door, "I'll get the staff started while we fill out the necessary paperwork. We should be able to have some imprinted checks and one of our special, solid gold credit cards ready for you before you leave."

"Hold it, Malcolm!"

Things were suddenly starting to move uncomfortably

fast, and I wanted a bit of clarification before they went much further.

The banker stopped as if he had hit the end of an invisible leash.

"Yes?"

"As you can probably tell, I'm not as at home with financial terms as I should be. Would you mind defining 'adequate financial support' to me . . . in layman's terms?"

The smile vanished as he licked his lips nervously.

"Well," he said, "we should be able to cover your day-to-day needs, but if you were to require substantial backing . . . say, over seven figures, we'd probably appreciate a day's warning."

Seven figures! He was saying the bank was ready to supply me with up to ten million . . . more if I gave them warning. I resolved that when I got back to the office, I was going to have to have Bunny go over our exact financial condition with me!

Chapter Sixteen:

"You can judge the success of a man by his
   bodyguards!"

—PRINCE

EDVIK WAS VISIBLY impressed by my success with the
bank. That was all right. I was impressed, too.

"Gee! A solid gold card! I've heard about those, but I've
never really seen one before," he exclaimed as I proudly
displayed my prize. "Not bad for a guy who didn't think
the bankers would want to even talk to him."

"It's my first time to deal with a bank," I said loftily.
"To be honest with you, I didn't even know about credit
cards until Malcolm explained them to me."

A cloud passed over the cabbie's face.

"You've never had a credit card before? Well, watch
your step is all I can say. They can be a dangerous habit,
and if you get behind, bankers can be worse than Deveels
to deal with."

"Worse than Deveels?"

I didn't like the sound of that. Deveels were a devil I
knew . . . if you'll pardon the pun. Now I was starting to
wonder if I should have asked a few more questions before

accepting the bank's services.

"Don't worry about it," Edvick said, giving my back a hearty slap. "With your money, you can't go wrong. Now then, let's see about finding you a bodyguard."

"Um . . . excuse me, but something just occurred to me."

"What's that?"

"Well, now that I have checks and a credit card, I don't have to carry a lot of cash around."

"Yeah. So?"

"So if I'm not carrying a lot of cash, what do I need a bodyguard for?" The cabbie rubbed his chin thoughtfully before answering.

"First of all, just because you and I and the bank know you aren't carrying a big wad anymore doesn't mean the muggers know it."

"Good point. I . . ."

"Then again, there's the gang that might still be after you for roughing them up last night . . ."

"Okay. Why don't we . . ."

" . . . And there's still an ax murderer loose somewhere around your hotel . . ."

"Enough! I get the picture! Let's go find a bodyguard."

It occurred to me that if I listened to Edvick long enough, I'd either want more than one bodyguard or decide not to set foot outside my room at all.

"Good," my guide declared, rubbing his hands together as the cab commenced its now familiar swerving. "I think I know just the person."

Settling back in my seat, it occurred to me that Edvick would probably get a kickback from this bodyguard he was lining me up with. That would explain his enthusiasm to get us together. I banished the thought as a needless suspicion.

The alert reader may have noticed that with the exception

of a vague reference to the fat lady in the department store, I have said absolutely nothing about female Pervects. There's a reason for that. Frankly, they intimidate me.

Now don't get me wrong, male Pervects are quite fearsome, as can be ascertained by my accounts of my friend and partner, Aahz. On the whole, they are big and muscular and would just as soon break you in two as look at you. Still, they possess a certain rough and tumble sense of humor, and are not above blustering a bit. All in all, they remind me of a certain type of lizard: the kind that puffs itself up and hisses when it's threatened . . . it can give a nasty bite, but it would probably prefer you to back down.

Female Pervects seem to be cut from a whole different bolt of cloth. Their eyes are narrower and set further back on the head, making them look more . . . well, reptilian. They never smile or laugh, and they don't *ever* bluff. In short, they look and act more dangerous than their male counterparts.

Some of you may wonder why I am choosing this point of the narrative to expound on the subject of female Pervects. The rest of you have already figured it out. For the former, let it suffice to say that the bodyguard Edvick introduced me to was a female.

We found her in a bar, a lounge, actually, which the cabbie informed me she used as an office between jobs. She didn't move or blink as we approached her table, which I came to realize meant she had been watching us from the moment we walked through the door. Edvick slid into a vacant chair at her table without invitation and motioned me into another.

"This is Skeeve . . . the Klahd I was telling you about," he announced, then turned to me. "Skeeve, this here's the bodyguard I'd recommend for you. There may be some better at doing what she does, but if so, I don't know 'em.

For protection against physical or magikal attacks, she's top
of the line.''

   With that, he leaned back in his chair, letting us size each
other up like two predators meeting over a fresh kill.

   Female Pervects seem to come in two body types. I'll
tell you about the other type later, but the kind the bodyguard
was was the lean, wiry variety. Even sitting down I could
tell she was tall, taller than me, anyway. Where Pervish
males, as typified by Aahz, were generally built like walls,
she was as slender and supple as a whip . . . a rapier to
their ax. I've mentioned that the men reminded me of lizards,
well, she made me think of a poisonous snake . . . graceful
and beautiful without being attractive. She was wearing a
dark waist-length cape that was almost a poncho except it
was open in front, revealing a form-fitting jumpsuit under-
neath. Even a violence know-nothing like me could tell the
cape would be perfect for producing and vanishing weapons
with unsettling ease. Overall, she impressed me as being
the most deadly woman I had ever met . . . realizing I
haven't met that many green, bald, scaly women.

   ''I hear you drink,'' she said bluntly, breaking the silence.

   ''Not well . . . and, after last night, not often,'' I returned.

   That earned me a curt nod.

   ''Good. A girl's got to watch her reputation.''

   It never even occurred to me that she might be referring
to her way with me. She was stating quite simply that if
anything happened to me while she was on guard, her professional status would suffer. What's more, she didn't want
to risk that reputation on a fool. As one inclined to talk too
much, I was impressed with how much she could communi-
cate with so few words.

   ''Ever work with a bodyguard before?''

   ''Yes. I have two back on Deva. They were . . . busy
elsewhere, so I came to Perv alone.''

There was a flicker in her eye and a slight tightening of her lips, which was as close as she came to expressing her opinion of bodyguards who let their principal come to Perv unescorted, then she continued with the subject at hand.

"Good. That means you already know the basic drill. The way I work, I go where you go and sleep where you sleep. I go through any door ahead of you unless I'm covering your exit, and I taste everything before you put it in your mouth. Clear?"

"I don't think you have to worry about poison on this one," Edvick said, "just muggers and . . . "

She cut him off with a glance.

"If he pays for the full treatment, he gets the full treatment. Clear, Skeeve?"

"On covering my exit . . . how do we handle it if we don't know what's on the other side of the door?"

I was thinking of how I got mousetrapped sneaking out of the last bar I was in.

"I cover you as far as the door, then you stand beside me while I check the exit. If there's trouble, I'll tell you which way to move . . . in or out."

"Clear."

"Any other questions?"

"Just if you'll be available for anywhere from a few days to a week," I said. "If so, I'd like to retain your services."

"Don't you want to know what I charge?"

I shrugged. "Why? I'm impressed. I'm ready to pay whatever it costs." I paused, then smiled. "Besides, you don't strike me as the type to either up the cost for a well-heeled client or to haggle over prices."

That earned me a brief, flat stare.

"I'll take the job," she said finally. "And you're right. I don't haggle *or* pad the bill. Those are two of my more endearing traits."

I wasn't sure if that last was intended as a joke or not, but decided it was as close as she was apt to get, and chuckled appreciatively.

"One more thing . . . what's your name?"

"Pookanthimbusille."

"Excuse me?" I blinked.

She gave a small shrug.

"Just call me Pookie. It's easier."

"Pookie?"

At first it struck me as a ridiculously silly name for her. Then I ran my eyes over her again, and allowed as how she could be called anything she wanted to be called. If anyone laughed, it wouldn't be me.

"Pookie it is then . . . just checking to be sure I had the pronunciation right. Shall we go?"

I had Edvick drive us back to the hotel. While I hadn't gotten a lot accomplished today toward finding Aahz, what I had done had left me feeling a little drained. Besides, there was another little matter I wanted to take care of.

For a change, luck seemed to be with me. As the cab pulled up in front of the hotel I could see J.R. at his usual place by the entrance. I figured that was fortunate since I wouldn't have known where to find him otherwise. I caught his eye through the window and waved him over. Unfortunately, Pookie *didn't* see me wave. All she saw was a street vendor moving to intercept us as we emerged from the cab.

"Pookie! NO!"

I was barely in time.

My bodyguard had a sinister looking weapon out and was drawing a bead on J.R. almost before I could say anything. At the sound of my warning, however, all movement froze and she shot me a vaguely quizzical look.

"It's all right," I said hastily. "He's a friend of mine. He's coming over because I waved at him as we pulled up."

The weapon vanished as she gave the street vendor a hard, appraising look.

"Interesting friends you have."

"He was the one who saved my bacon in last night's encounter with the local wildlife. Hang on a few . . . I've got a little business to transact with him."

Pookie nodded and began scanning the immediate area with a watchful eye as I turned to J.R.

"Interesting friends you've got," he said, staring at my bodyguard.

"Funny, she was just saying the same thing about you. She's my new bodyguard. After last night, it seemed like a good idea. Incidentally, sorry about that welcome. I forgot to warn her you were coming over."

"No problem. What's up?"

"I paid a little visit to the bank today," I explained, holding up my checkbook. "Now I've got the funding for that little venture of ours."

"Hey! That's terrific! That's all I need to start making us some *real* money."

"Not so fast," I cautioned. "Let's settle the details and paper this thing first."

"What for? You've already said you trust me and I sure trust you."

"It's cleaner this way. Contracts are the best way to be sure we're both hearing the same thing in this arrangement . . . not to mention it documents the split at the beginning instead of waiting until we're arguing over a pile of profits."

He was still a bit reluctant, but I managed to convince him and we scribbled down the details in duplicate on some pieces of paper he produced from one of his many pockets. I say 'we' because I couldn't read or write Pervish, and he was equally ignorant of Klahdish, so we each had to make two copies of the agreement in our own language. To say

the least, I didn't drive a particularly hard bargain . . . 25%
of the profits after expenses. I figured he would be doing
all of the work, so he should get the bulk of the reward.
All I was doing was funding him. I even put in a clause
where he could buy out my share if things went well. When
it was done, we each signed all the copies and shook hands.

"Thanks, Skeeve," the vendor beamed, stuffing one copy
of each translation into a pocket. "Believe me, this is a
sure money maker."

"Any idea yet where your storefront is going to be?"

"No. Remember I said I was going to start out small?
Well, I figure to start by supplying the other street vendors,
then using the profits from that to lease and stock the storefront. It'll probably be three weeks to a month before I'm
ready for that move."

A month wasn't too bad for start-up time. I admired his
industry and confidence.

"Well, good luck!" I said sincerely. "Be sure to leave
word for me at the bank when you have a permanent address.
I'll be in touch."

He gathered his wares and headed off down the street as
I joined Pookie once more.

"I'd like to apologize for that mix-up," I said. "I should
have let you know he was coming over."

"I figured he was okay," the bodyguard replied, still
watching the street. "He didn't move like a mugger. It just
seemed like a good time for a little demonstration, so I did
my thing."

"You really didn't have to put on a demonstration for
me. I don't have any doubts about your abilities."

Pookie glanced at me.

"Not for you," she corrected. "For them . . . the folks
watching here on the street. It was my way of announcing

that you're covered now and they should keep their distance.''

That possibility had never occurred to me.

"Oh," I said. "Well, I guess I should stick with my business and let you handle yours."

"Agreed," she nodded, "though I'll admit the way you do business puzzles me a bit. Sorry, but I couldn't help but overhear your dealings there."

"What? You mean my insisting on a contract? The reason I pushed for it there and not for *our* deal is that it was a long-term investment as opposed to a straight-forward purchase of services."

"That isn't it."

"What is it then . . . the contract terms? Maybe I was a little more generous than I had to be, but the situation is . . ."

I broke off as I realized the bodyguard was staring hard at me.

"What I meant," she said flatly, "was that before I put money into a business, I'd want to know what it was."

"You heard him. It's a wholesale/dealer operation."

"Yes, but what's he selling?"

I didn't answer that one because I didn't *have* an answer. In my eagerness to do J.R. a good turn, I had completely forgotten to ask what kind of business he was starting!

Chapter Seventeen:

"Bibbity . . . bobbity . . ."

—S. STRANGE, M.D.

BRIGHT AND EARLY the next morning, I launched into the next phase of my search for Aahz. The Butterfly had convinced me it was unlikely I'd find him traveling in financial circles. That left the magicians.

As Edvick had warned, the sheer volume of Pervects in the magik business made the task seem almost impossible. It was my last idea, though, so I had to give it a try and hope I got lucky. By the time I had visited half a dozen or so operations, however, I was nearly ready to admit I was licked.

The *real* problem facing me was that the market glut had made the magicians extremely competitive. No one was willing to talk about any other magicians, or even acknowledge their existence. What I got was high-powered sales pitches and lectures on "the layman's need for magikal assistance in his day-to-day life". Once I admitted I was in the business myself, I either got offered a partnership or was accused of spying and thrown out of the office. (Well, a couple of them threatened, but thanks to Pookie's presence I got to walk out with dignity.) What I *didn't* get was any leads or information about Aahz.

Despite my growing despair of succeeding with my quest, it was interesting to view magikal hype as an outsider. Kalvin had admonished me for being too insecure and downplaying my abilities. What I learned that day after sitting through several rounds of bragging in close succession, was that the louder someone blew his own horn, the less impressed the listener, in this case, me, was apt to be. I thought of the quiet confidence exuded by people such as the Butterfly and Pookie, and decided that, in general, that was a much wiser way to conduct oneself in business situations . . . or social ones for that matter. As far as I could tell, the goal was not to impress people, but rather to *be* impressive. In line with that, I resolved to not only discourage the "Mister Skeeve" title, but to also drop "The Great Skeeve" hype. I had never really believed it anyway. What I was was "Skeeve," and people could either be impressed or not by what I was, not by what I called myself.

If this seems like a sudden bolt from the blue to you, it isn't. The area of Perv I was covering was large enough that I was spending considerable time riding back and forth in Edvick's taxi, and it gave me lots of time to think and reflect on what I was seeing and hearing. What's more, the advice given me by the Butterfly and Kalvin, not to mention the questions I had to ask myself about trying to fetch Aahz, had given me cause to reexamine my own attitudes and priorities, so I had plenty to think about.

Dealing with what seemed to be an endless parade of people who had never heard of me before, much less met me, gave me a unique chance to observe how people interacted. More and more I found myself reflecting on how I reacted to them and they reacted to me.

Pervects had a reputation for being nasty and vicious, not to mention arrogant. There was also ample evidence that they could be more than slightly rude. Still, I had also encountered individuals who had been helpful and gentle, such as the Butterfly, and even those like J.R. who would risk themselves physically for a near stranger who was in trouble. Clearly there was danger in stereotyping people, though it was interesting to observe the behavior patterns which had developed to deal with a crowded, competitive environment. Even more interesting was noting those who seemed immune to the environmental pressure that ruled the others about them.

The more I thought about it, the more I began to see pieces of myself reflected in the Pervish behavior. Kalvin had commented on my actively trying to be strong . . . of being cold and ruthless in an effort to hide my own feared weaknesses. Was it all that different with the blustering Pervects who would rather shout than admit they might be wrong? Were my own feelings of insecurity and inadequacy making me insensitive and closed to the very people who could help me?

The thought was enough to inspire me to voice my frustrations to Edvick and ask if he had any thoughts as to alternate methods of searching the magikal community.

"I was just thinking about that, Skeeve," he said over his shoulder, "but I didn't figure it was my place to say anything unless you asked."

"Well, I'm asking. After all, there's no shame in admitting you know this dimension better than I do."

That last was said as much to myself as to Edvick, but the cabbie accepted it in stride.

"Too true. Well, what I was thinking was that instead of working to get magicians to talk about potential competitors, maybe you should try checking the schools."

"The schools?"

"Sure. You know, the places that teach these spell-slingers their trade. They should have some kind of records showing who's learned what. What's more, they should be willing to share them since you're not a competitor."

That made sense, but it seemed almost too easy.

"Even if that's true, do you think they would bother to keep current addresses on their old students?"

"Are you kidding?" the cabbie laughed. "How else could the old Alma Mater be able to solicit donations from their alumni? This may not be Deva, but do you think a Pervect would lose track of a revenue source?"

I felt my hope being renewed as he spoke.

"That's a great idea, Edvick! How many magik schools are there, anyway?"

"Not more than a dozen or so of any note. Nowhere near the number of businesses. If I were you, I'd start with the biggest and work your way down."

"Then that's what we'll do. Take me to the top of the list and don't spare the lizards . . . and Edvick? Thanks."

The grounds of the Magikal Institute of Perv (MIP) occupied an entire city block. I say grounds because much of it was well trimmed lawns and bushes, a marked contrast to the closely packed buildings and alleys that seemed to compose the majority of Perv. Stately old buildings of brick or stone were scattered here and there, apparently oblivious to the bustling metropolis that screeched and honked scant yards from their tranquility. Looking at them, one could almost read their stoic thoughts: that if they ignored it long enough, maybe the rest of the world would go away.

There was an iron fence surrounding the school in token protection from intrusion, but the gate stood wide open. I peered out the windows of the cab in curiosity as we drove up to what Edvick said was the administration building, hoping to catch a glimpse of the students practicing their lessons, but was disappointed. The people I saw were much more interested in being young—skylarking and flirting with each other—than in demonstrating their learning to a casual visitor. I did, however, notice there were more than a few students from off-dimension in their number. Either the school was much more tolerant of off-worlders than the rest of the dimension, or they simply weren't as picky about who they accepted money from. I never did get a chance to find out which it really was.

After a few inquiries, I was shown into the office of the head record keeper. That individual listened carefully to my story, though he was so still and outwardly calm that I found myself fighting a temptation to make a face at him in mid-sentence just to see if he was really paying attention. I have a hunch I would not do well in a formal educational environment.

"I see," he said, once I had ground to a halt. "Well, your request seems reasonable. Aahz . . . Aahz . . . I don't recall the name off-hand, but it does ring some sort of a bell. Oh well, we can check it easily enough. GRETTA!?"

In response to his call, a young female Pervect appeared in the office door. She glanced quickly at Pookie who was leaning against the wall behind me, but except for that ignored my bodyguard as completely as the record keeper had.

"Yes sir?"

"Gretta, this is Mr. Skeeve. He's trying to locate someone who might have been a student here. I'd like you to help him locate the appropriate file in the archives . . . if it exists. Mr. Skeeve, this is Gretta. She's one of the apprentices here who helps us . . . is something wrong?"

I had suddenly drawn back the hand I had been extending to shake hands with Gretta, and the record keeper had noted the move.

"Oh, nothing . . . really," I said embarrassed. I quickly reached out and shook the offered hand. "It's a . . . bad habit I learned from Aahz. I really should break it. You were saying?"

The record keeper ignored my efforts to cover the social gaff.

"What bad habit is that?"

"It's silly, but . . . Well, Aahz, back when he was my teacher, wouldn't shake hands with me once I became his apprentice. When we first met and after we became partners it was okay, but not while I was his student. I don't shake hands with apprentices he used to say . . . only louder. I hadn't realized I had picked it up until just now. Sorry, Gretta. Nothing personal."

"Of course . . . Aahzmandius!"

The record keeper seemed suddenly excited.

"Excuse me?" I said, puzzled.

"Gretta, this won't require a file search after all. Bring me the file on Aahzmandius . . . it will be in the dropout file . . . three or four centuries back if I recall correctly."

Once the apprentice had scampered off, the record keeper returned his attention to me once more.

"I'm sorry, Mr. Skeeve. I just managed to recall the individual you're looking for. Refusing to shake hands with apprentices was the tipoff. It was one of his least objectionable quirks. Aahzmandius! After all these years I can still remember him."

After searching so long I was reluctant to believe my luck.

"Are you sure we're talking about the same person? Aahz?"

"Oh my, yes. That's why the name rang a bell. Aahz

was the nickname Aahzmandius would use when he was exercising his dubious love of practical jokes . . . or doing anything else he didn't want reflected on his permanent record, for that matter. There was a time when that name would strike terror into the hearts of any under-classman on campus.''

"I take it he wasn't a particularly good student?" I said, trying to hide my grin.

"Oh, on the contrary, he was one of the brightest students we've ever had here. That's much of why the faculty and administration were willing to overlook the . . . um, less social aspects of his character. He was at the head of his class while he was here, and everyone assumed a bright future for him. I'm not sure he was aware of it, but long before he was slated to graduate, there was a raging debate going on about him among the faculty. One side felt that every effort should be made to secure him a position with the institute as an instructor after he graduated. The other felt that with his arrogant distaste for inferiors, placing him in constant contact with students would . . . well, let's just say they felt his temperament would be better suited to private practice, and the school could benefit best by simply accepting his financial contributions as an alumni . . . preferably mailed from far away.''

I was enthralled by this new insight into Aahz's background. However, I could not help but note there was something that didn't seem to fit with the record keeper's oration.

"Excuse me," I said, "but didn't I hear you tell Gretta to look in the dropout file for Aahz's records? If he was doing so well, why didn't he graduate?"

The Pervect heaved a great sigh, a look of genuine pain on his face.

"His family lost their money in a series of bad investments. With his financial support cut off, he dropped out of school . . . left quietly in the middle of a semester even though his tuition had been paid in full for the entire term. We offered him a scholarship so that he could complete his education . . . there was even a special meeting held specifically to get the necessary approvals so he wouldn't be kept dangling until the scholarship board would normally convene. He wouldn't accept it, though. It's a shame, really. He had such potential.''

"That doesn't sound like the Aahz I know," I frowned. "I've never known him to refuse money. Usually, he wouldn't even wait for it to be offered . . . not nailing it down would be considered enough of an invitation for him to help himself. Did he give any reason for not accepting the scholarship?''

"No, but it was easy enough to understand at the time. His family had been quite well off, you see, and he had lorded his wealth over the less fortunate as much or more than he had harassed them with his superior abilities. I think he left school because he couldn't bear to face his old cronies, much less his old victims, in his new cash poor condition. Basically, he was too proud to be a scholarship student after having established himself as a campus aristocrat. Aahzmandius may not refuse money, but I think you'll find he has an aversion to charity . . . or anything that might be construed as such.''

It all made sense. The portrait he was painting of Aahz, or as he was known here, Aahzmandius, seemed to confirm the Butterfly's analysis of my old mentor's financial habits. If he had suffered from embarrassment and seen his plans for the future ruined because of careless money management, it stood to reason that he would respond by becoming ultraconservative if not flat out miserly when it came to accumulating and protecting our cache of hard cash.

"Ah! Here we are.''

I was pulled out of my musings by the record keeper's exclamation at Gretta's return. I felt my anticipation rise as he took the offered folder and began perusing its contents. For the first time since arriving on Perv, I was going to have a solid lead on how to find Aahz. Then I noticed he was frowning.

"What's wrong?"

"I'm sorry, Mr. Skeeve," the record keeper said, glancing up from the folder. "It seems we don't have a current address for your associate. The note here says 'Traveling.' I guess that, realizing his financial situation, we haven't been as diligent about keeping track of him as we've been with our other alumni."

I fought against a wave of disappointment, unwilling to believe that after everything I had been through, this was going to turn out to be another dead end.

"Didn't he have a school or business or something? I met one of his apprentices once."

The Pervect shook his head.

"No. That we would have known about. He may have been willing to instruct a few close friends or relatives . . . that's not uncommon for someone who's studied here. But I think I can say for sure that he hasn't been doing any formal teaching here or on any other dimension. We would have heard, if for no other reason than his students would have contacted us to confirm his credentials."

Now that he mentioned it, I did recall that Rupert, the apprentice I had met, had specifically been introduced as Aahz's nephew. Overcome with a feeling of hopelessness, I almost missed what the record keeper said next.

"Speaking of relatives. We *do* have an address for his next of kin . . . in this case, his mother. Perhaps if you spoke to her, you might find out his current whereabouts."

Chapter Eighteen:

" 'M' is for the many things she taught me . . . "
—OEDIPUS

THE SEARCH FOR the address the record keeper had given me led us onto some of the dimension's side streets which made up the residential areas. Though at first Perv seems to be composed entirely of businesses, there is also a thriving neighborhood community just a few steps off the main business and transportation drags.

I'll admit to not being thrilled by the neighborhood Aahz's mother lived in once we found it. Not that it looked particularly rough or dirty . . . . at least no dirtier than the rest of the dimension. It's just that it was . . . well, shabby. The buildings and streets were so run-down that I found it depressing to think anyone, much less the mother of a friend of mine, would live there.

"I'll wait for you here on the street," Pookie announced as I emerged from the taxi.

I looked at her, surprised.

"Aren't you coming in?"

"I figure it's more important to guard your escape route,"

she said. "I don't think there's any danger inside, unless the place falls down when you knock on the door . . . and I couldn't help there anyway. Why? Are you expecting more trouble than you can handle from one old lady?"

Since I didn't have a snappy retort for that, I proceeded up the porch steps to the door. There was a list of names with a row of buttons beside them. I found the name of Aahz's mother with no difficulty, and pressed the button next to it.

A few moments later, a voice suddenly rasped from the wall next to my elbow.

"Who is it?"

It only took a few seconds for me to figure out that it was some kind of speaker system.

"It's . . . I'm a friend of your son, Aahz . . . Aahzmandius, that is. I was wondering if I might talk to you for a few moments?"

There was a long pause before the reply came back.

"I suppose if you're already here I might as well talk to you. Come right up."

There was a sudden raucous buzzing at the door. I waited patiently, and in a few moments it stopped. I continued waiting.

"Are you still down there?"

"Yes, Ma'am."

"Why?"

"Excuse me?"

"Why didn't you open the door and come in when I buzzed you through?"

"Oh, is that what that was? I'm sorry, I didn't know. Could you . . . buzz me through again?"

"What's the matter, haven't you ever seen a remote lock before?"

I suppose it was meant as a rhetorical question, but my

annoyance at being embarrassed prompted me to answer.

"As a matter of fact, I haven't. I'm just visiting this dimension. We don't have anything like it back on Klah."

. There was a long silence, long enough for me to wonder if it had been a mistake to admit I was from off-dimension. The buzzer went off, somehow catching me unaware again even though I had been expecting it.

This time, I managed to get the door open before the buzzing stopped, and stepped through into the vestibule. The lighting was dim, and got downright dark after I let the door shut. I started to open it again to get my bearings, but pulled my hand back at the last minute. It might set off an alarm somewhere, and if there was one thing I didn't need right now it was more trouble.

Slowly my eyes adjusted to the shadowy dimness, and I could make out a narrow hall with an even narrower flight of stairs which vanished into the gloom above. "Come right up" she had said, so I took her literally and started up the stairs . . . hoping all the while I was right.

After ascending several flights, this hope was becoming fervent. There was no sign of habitation on any of the halls I passed, and the way the stairs creaked and groaned under me, I wasn't at all sure I wasn't heading into a condemned area of the building.

Just when I was about to yield to my fears and retreat to the ground floor, the stairs ended. The apartment I was looking for was right across the hall from where I stood, so I had little choice but to proceed. Raising my hand, I knocked gently, afraid that anything more violent might trigger a catastrophic chain reaction.

"Come in! It's open!"

Summoning my courage, I let myself in.

The place was both tiny and jammed with clutter. I had the impression one could reach out one's arms and touch the opposing walls simultaneously. In fact, I had to fight against the impulse to do exactly that, as the walls and their contents appeared to be on the brink of caving in. I think it was then I discovered that I was mildly claustrophobic.

"So you're a friend of that no-account Aahzmandius. I knew he'd come to no good, but I never dreamed he'd sink so low as to hang around with a Klahd."

This last was uttered by what had to be Aahz's mother . . . it had to be because she was the only person in the room besides myself! My eye had passed over her at first, she was so much a part of the apartment, but once she drew my attention, she seemed to dominate the entire environ . . . if not the whole dimension.

Remember when I said that Pookie was one of two types of females I had noted on Perv? Well, Aahz's mother was the other type. While Pookie was sleek and muscular in an almost serpentine way, the figure before me resembled nothing so much as a huge toad . . . a green, scaly, reptilian toad. (I have since had it pointed out to me that toads are amphibians and not reptiles, but at the time that's what she made me think of.)

She was dressed in a baggy housecoat which made her seem even more bloated than she really was. The low, stuffed chair she was sitting in was almost obscured from view by her bulk, which seemed to swell over the sides of the chair and flow onto the mottled carpet. There was a tangle of white string on her lap which she jabbed at viciously with a small, barbed stick she was holding. At first, it gave the illusion she was torturing string, but then I noticed there were similar masses draped over nearly every available flat surface in the apartment, and concluded that she was involved in some kind of craft project, the nature of which was beyond my knowledge or appreciation.

"Good afternoon, Mrs. . . . ."

"Call me Duchess," she snapped. "Everyone does. Don't know why, though . . . haven't had royalty on this dimension for generations. Beheaded them all and divvied up their property . . . those were the days!"

She smacked her lips at the memory, though of royalty or beheadings I wasn't sure, and pointed vaguely at the far wall. I looked, half expecting to see a head mounted on a plaque, then realized she was pointing at a faded picture hanging there. I also realized I couldn't make it out through the dust and grime on its surface.

"It's the maid's day off," the Duchess said sharply, noting my expression. "Can't get decent work out of domestics since they outlawed flogging!"

I have seldom heard such an obvious lie . . . about the maid, I mean, not the flogging. The cobwebs, dust, and litter which were prevalent everywhere could not have accumulated in a day . . . or in a year for that matter. The shelves and cases throughout the room were jammed with the tackiest collection of bric-a-brac and dustcatchers it had ever been my misfortune to behold, and every dustcatcher had caught its capacity and more. I had no idea why the Duchess felt it necessary to imply she had servants when she obviously had little regard for me, but there was no point in letting her know I didn't believe her.

"Yes. Well . . . Duchess, I've been trying to locate your son, Aahz . . . mandius, and was hoping you might have some information as to his whereabouts."

"Aahzmandius? That wastrel?" Her narrow yellow eyes seemed to glow angrily. "If I had any idea where he was, do you think I'd be sitting here?"

"Wastrel?"

I was starting to wonder if we were talking about the same Aahz.

"What would you call it?" she snapped. "He hasn't sent

me a cent since he left school. That means he's spending so much on himself there's nothing left to share with the family that nurtured him and raised him and made him what he is today. How does he expect me to maintain the lifestyle expected of our family, much less keep up my investing, if he doesn't send me any money?''

"Investing?" I said, the light starting to dawn.

"Of course. I've been doing all the investing for our family since my husband passed on. I was just starting to get the hang of it when Aahzmandius quit school and disappeared without a cent . . . I mean a trace. I'm sure that if I just had a few million more to work with I'd get it right this time.''

"I see.''

"Say, you wouldn't by any chance have access to some venture capital, would you? I could invest it for you and we could split the profits . . . except it's best to put your money to work by reinvesting it as soon as you get it.''

I was suddenly very aware of the weight of the checkbook in my pocket. The conversation was taking a decidedly uncomfortable turn.

"Um . . . actually I'm a little short right now," I hedged. "In fact, I was looking for . . . Aahzmandius because he owes me money.''

"Well, don't you have any friends you could borrow a million or two from?''

"Not really. They're all as poor as I am. In fact, I've got to go now, Duchess. I've got a cab waiting downstairs and every minute I'm here is costing more than you'd imagine.''

I suppose I should have been despairing as Edvick drove Pookie and me back to the hotel. My last hope for finding Aahz was gone. Now that tracking him down through the magicians had proved to be futile, I had no idea how to locate him other than knocking on every door in the dimension . . . and I just didn't have the energy to attempt that even if I had the time. The mission was a bust, and there was nothing to do but pay off Edvick and Pookie, check out of the hotel, and figure out how to signal Massha to pick me up and take me to Klah. I hoped that simply removing the ring she had given me would bring her running, but I wasn't sure. Maybe I would be more effective at stopping Queen Hemlock than I had been in finding Aahz. I *should* have been despairing as I wrote out the checks for my driver and bodyguard in preparation for our parting, but I wasn't. Instead, I found myself thinking about the Duchess.

My first reaction to her was that she was a crazy old lady trying to live in the past by maintaining an illusion of wealth that nobody believed except her. Ideally, someone who cared should give her a stern talking to and try to bring her back into contact with reality so she could start adjusting to what *was* instead of what *had been* or *should be*. I guess, on reflection, I found her situation to be more sad than irritating or contemptible.

Then, somehow, my thoughts began wandering from her case to my own. Was I as guilty as she was of trying to run my life on *was* and *should be* instead of accepting and dealing with reality? I *had been* an untraveled, untrained youth, and that self-image still haunted me in everything I said and did. I felt I *should be* a flawless businessman and manager, and treated both myself and others rather harshly pursuing that goal. What was my *reality*?

Even before coming to Perv, many of my associates, including Aahz, had tried to convince me I was something more than I felt I was. Time and time again, I had discounted their words, assuming they were either trying to be nice to 'the Kid', or, in some cases, trying to badger me into growing up faster than I was ready to.

Well, maybe it was time I decided I *was* ready to grow up, mentally at least. The physical part would take care of itself. One by one, I started knocking down the excuses that had been my protective wall for so long.

Okay, I was young and inexperienced. So what? "Inexperienced" wasn't the same as "stupid." There was no reason to expect myself to be adept or even familiar with situations and concepts I had never encountered before. It was crucial not to dwell on my shortcomings. What *was* important was that I was learning, and learning fast . . . Fast enough that even my critics and enemies showed a certain degree of grudging admiration for what I was. They, like the Pervects I had encountered on this mission, didn't care what I didn't know last year or what I still had to learn, they reacted to what I was now. Shouldn't I be doing the same thing?

Speaking of learning, I had always been self-conscious about what I didn't know, yet I planned to keep on learning my whole life. I always figured that if I ever stopped learning, it would either mean that I had closed my mind, or that I was dead. Putting those two thoughts together, it occurred to me that in being ashamed of what I didn't know, I was effectively apologizing for being alive! Of course there were things I didn't know! So what? That didn't make me an outsider or a freak, it gave me something in common with everyone else who was alive. Instead of wasting my energy bemoaning what I didn't know, I should be using what I *did* know to expand my own horizons.

The phrase "Today is the first day of the rest of your life" was almost a cliché across the dimensions. It occurred to me that a better phrasing would be "Your whole life to date has been training for right now!" The question wasn't what I had or didn't have so much as what I was going to do with it!

I was still examining this concept when we pulled up to the curb in front of the hotel.

"Here we are, Skeeve," Edvick said, swiveling around in his seat. "Are you sure you aren't going to need me anymore?"

"There's no point," I sighed, passing him his check. "I've run out of ideas and time. I'd like to thank you for your help, though. You've been much more than a driver and guide to me during my stay here. I've added a little extra onto the check as a bit more tangible expression of my gratitude."

Actually I had added a *lot* more onto it. The cabbie glanced at the figure and beamed happily.

"Hey, thanks, Skeeve. I'm sorry you couldn't find your friend."

"That's the way it goes sometimes," I shrugged. "Take care of yourself, Edvick. If you ever make it to Deva, look me up and I'll show you around *my* dimension for a change."

"I just might take you up on that," the cabbie waved as I let myself out onto the street.

Pookie had popped out of the taxi as soon as we stopped, so it seemed I was going to have to settle accounts with her out in the open.

"Pookie, I . . . "

"Heads up, Skeeve," she murmured, not looking at me. "I think we've got problems."

I followed her gaze with my eyes. Two uniformed policemen were bracketing the door to my hotel. At the sight of me, they started forward with expressions of grim determination on their faces.

Chapter Nineteen:

"I am not a crook!"

—ANY CROOK

"ZAT EES HEEM! Ze third from ze right!"

Even with the floodlights full in my face, I had no difficulty recognizing the voice which floated up to me from the unseen area in the room beyond the lights. It was the waiter I had clashed with the first night I was on Perv. The one who claimed I had tried to avoid paying for my meal by fainting.

I wasn't surprised by his ability to identify me in the lineup. First of all, I had no reason to suspect his powers of observation and recall were lacking. More important, of all the individuals in the line up, I was the only one who wasn't a Pervect. What's more, all the others were uniformed policemen! Nothing like a nice, impartial setup, and this was just that . . . nothing like a nice, impartial setup.

What *did* surprise me was that I didn't seem to be the least bit upset by the situation. Usually, in a crisis like this, I would either be extremely upset or too angry to care. This time, however, I simply felt a bit bemused. In fact, I felt

181

so relaxed and in control of myself and the situation, I decided to have a bit of fun with it . . . just to break the monotony.

"Look again, sir. Are you absolutely sure?"

I knew that voice, too. It was the captain who had given J.R. and me so much grief the last time I had the pleasure of enjoying police hospitality. Before the waiter could respond, I used my disguise spell and switched places with the policeman standing next to me.

"I am sure. He ees the third . . . no, the second from the right!"

"What?"

Resisting the urge to grin, I went to work again, this time changing everyone in the lineup so they were identical images of me.

"But . . . but thees ees imposs-ible!"

"MISTER Skeeve. If you don't mind?"

"Excuse me, captain?" I said innocently.

"We'd appreciate it a lot if you'd quit playing games with the witnesses!"

"That makes us even," I smiled. "I'd appreciate it if you quit playing games with me! However, I think I've made my point."

I let the disguise spell drop, leaving the policemen in the lineup to glare suspiciously at each other as well as at me.

"What point is that?"

"That this whole lineup thing is silly. We'll ignore the bit with putting all of your colleagues up here with me for the moment and assume you were playing it straight. My point is that I'm not the only one who knows how to use a disguise spell. Anyone who's laid eyes on me or seen a picture of me could use a disguise spell well enough to fool the average witness. That invalidates the lineup identification as evidence. All you've established is that someone with access to my image has been seen by the witness . . . not that I personally, was anywhere near him."

There was a long silence beyond the lights.

"You're denying having had any contact with the witness? I take it you recognize his voice."

"That's a rather transparent catch question, Captain," I laughed. "If I admit to recognizing his voice, then at the same time I'm admitting to having had contact with him. Right?"

I was starting to actually enjoy myself.

"As a matter of fact, I'm willing to admit I've had dealings with your witness there. Also with the doorman and bellhop, as well as the other people you've dragged in to identify me. I was just questioning the validity of your procedure. It seems to me that you're putting yourself and everyone else through a lot of trouble that, by itself, won't yield any usable results. If you want information about me and my movements, why don't you just ask me directly instead of going through all this foolishness?"

The floodlights went out suddenly, leaving me even more blinded than when they had been on.

"All right, *Mister* Skeeve. We'll try it your way. If you'll be so good as to follow me down to one of our 'interview' rooms?"

Even "trying it my way" was more hassle than I expected or liked. True, I was out from in front of the floodlights, but there were enough people crowded into the small "interview room" to make me feel like I was still on exhibition.

"Really, Captain," I said, sweeping the small crowd with my eyes. "Is all this really necessary?"

"As a matter of fact, it is," he retorted. "I want to have witnesses to everything you say as well as a transcript of our little conversation. I suppose I should inform you that anything you say can and may be used against you in court.

What's more, you're entitled to an attorney for advice during this questioning, either one of your choice or one of those on call to the court. Now, do we continue or shall we wait for a legal advisor?''

My feeling of control dimmed a bit. Somehow, this seemed much more serious than my last visit.

"Am I being charged with anything?"

"Not yet," the captain said. "We'll see how the questioning goes.''

I had been thinking of trying to get in touch with Shai-ster, one of the Mob's lawyers. It occurred to me, however, that just having access to him might damage the image I was attempting to project of an innocent, injured citizen.

"Then I'll give the questioning a shot on my own," I said. "I may holler for legal help if it get's too rough, though.''

"Suit yourself," the policeman shrugged, picking up the sheaf of papers he had brought in with him.

Something in his manner made me think I had just made the wrong choice in not insisting on having a lawyer. Nervously, I began to chatter, fishing for reassurance that things really weren't as bad as they were starting to seem.

"Actually, Captain, I'm a little surprised that I'm here. I thought we had covered everything pretty well my last visit.''

The police who had picked me up in front of my hotel and delivered me to the station had been extremely tight-lipped. Beyond the simple statement that "The captain wants to see you," they hadn't given the slightest indication of why I was being pulled in.

"Oh, the IDs were just to confirm we were dealing with the right person," the captain smiled. "A point you have very generously conceded. As to why you're here, it seems there are one or two minor things we didn't cover the last time we chatted."

He picked up one of the sheets, holding it by his fingertips as if it were extremely fragile or precious.

"You see, just as I promised, we've run a check on you through some of the other dimensions."

My confidence sank right along with my heart . . . deep into the pit of my stomach.

"For the record," the captain was saying, "you are Skeeve, sometimes known as 'the Great Skeeve' . . . originally from Klah with offices on Deva?"

"That's right."

"Now it seems you were somehow involved in a war a while back . . . somewhere around Possiltum?"

There was nothing for me to duck there.

"I was at that time employed as Court Magician of Possiltum. Helping to stop an invading army was simply a part of my duties."

"Really? I also have a report from Jahk that says you were part of a group that stole the Trophy from the Great Game. Was that part of your duties, too?"

"We won that fair and square in a challenge match," I flared. "The Jahks agreed to it in advance . . . and darn near beat our brains out before we won."

" . . . Which you did with much the same team as you used to stop the aforementioned invading army," the captain commented drily.

"They're friends of mine," I protested. "We work together from time to time, and help each other out when one of us gets in a jam."

"Uh-huh. Would you describe your relationship with the Mob the same way? You know, friends who work together and help each other out of jams from time to time?"

Whoops! There it was. Well, now that the subject was on the table, it was probably best to deal with it openly and honestly.

"That's different," I dodged.

"I'll say it is!" the captain snarled. "In fact, I don't think different begins to describe it! In all my years on the force I've never heard of anything like it!"

He scooped up a handful of paper and held it up dramatically.

"From Klah, we have conflicting reports. One source says that you were instrumental in keeping the Mob from moving in on Possiltum. Another has you down as being a sub-chieftan in the Mob itself!"

He grabbed another handful.

"That's particularly interesting, seeing as how Deva reports that you stopped the Mob from moving into *that* dimension. What's more, you're being paid a fat retainer to maintain the defenses against the Mob, even though it seems that much of that retainer is going toward paying off your staff . . . which includes two bodyguards from the Mob and the niece of the current head of the Mob! All of which, of course, has nothing to do with the fact that you own and operate a combination hotel and casino and are known to associate with gamblers and assassins. Just what kind of game are you playing, MISTER Skeeve? I'm dying to hear just how *you* define 'different!'"

I considered trying my best to explain the rather tangled set of relationships and circumstances that define my life just now. Then I considered saving my breath.

"First, let me check something here, Captain. Does your jurisdiction extend to other dimensions? To put it another way, is it any of your business what I do or don't do away from Perv, or did you just pull me in here to satisfy your curiosity?"

Pursing his lips, the Pervect set the papers he was holding back on the table and squared them very carefully.

"Oh, I'm *very* curious about you, *Mister* Skeeve," he said softly, "But that's not the reason I sent for you."

"Well then, can we get down to what the problem *really* is? As much as I'd like to entertain you with my life story, there are other rather pressing demands on my time."

The policeman stared at me stonily.

"All right. We'll stick to cases. Do you know a street vendor named J.R.?"

The sudden change of subject threw me off-stride.

"J.R.? Sure I know him. Don't you remember? The last time I was here he was sitting . . . "

"How would you describe your relationship with the individual in question?" the captain interrupted.

"I guess you'd say we're friends," I shrugged. "I've been chatting with him off and on since I arrived on Perv, and, as you know, he helped me out that time I got into a fight."

"Anything else?"

"No . . . except we're going into business together. That is, I've put up the money for a venture of his."

The captain seemed taken aback.

"You mean you admit it?" he said.

A little alarm started to ring in the back of my head.

"Sure. I mean, what's so unusual about a businessman investing in a new enterprise?"

"Wait a minute. What kind of an enterprise did you think you were buying into?"

"He said he was going to open a retail storefront," I said uneasily. "But he did say something about supplying the other street vendors for a while to build up his operating capital. Exactly *what* he was supplying I was never really sure."

"You weren't sure?"

"Well, the truth is I was in a hurry and forgot to ask. Why? What was he . . ."

"We just picked him up for smuggling! It seems your buddy and business partner was using your funds to buy and sell contraband!"

Needless to say, the news upset me. It had occurred to me that, in his enthusiasm, J.R. would go outside the law for the sake of quick profits.

"How serious is it, Captain? Can I post bail for him . . . or arrange for a lawyer?"

"Don't worry about him," the Pervect advised. "It turns out he has some information on the ax murderer we've been looking for and is willing to share it with us if we drop the smuggling charges. No, you should be more worried about yourself."

"ME?"

"That's right. You've admitted you're his partner in this, which makes you just as guilty as he is."

"But I didn't know what he was going to do! Honest!"

Now I *was* worried. The whole thing was absurd, but I was starting to think I should have insisted on having a lawyer after all.

"That's what you say," the captain said grimly. "Would you like to see what he was smuggling?"

He gestured at one of the other policemen in the room who held up several plastic bags with small items in them. I recognized them at a glance, a fact which did nothing for my peace of mind.

"Those are all products of the Acme Joke and Novelty Company," the captain intoned. "A company I believe you've worked with in the recent past?"

"A team of my employees did some work there on a pilferage case," I mumbled, not able to take my eyes off the items in the bags. "Are those things really illegal on Perv?"

"We have a lot of ordinances that try to keep the quality of life on Perv high. We haven't been able to stop porn, but we have managed to outlaw trashy, practical joke items like Rubber Doggie Doodle with Realistic Life-Like Aroma that Actually Sticks to Your Hand."

It seemed like a very minor achievement to me, considering the crime on the streets I had already been exposed to. I didn't think that it was wise to point this out just now, though.

"Okay, Captain, let me rephrase my question," I said, looking at the floor. "How much trouble am *I* in? I mean, what's really involved here . . . a fine, a jail term, what?"

The Pervect was so silent I finally raised my head to meet his gaze directly. He was looking at me with a flat, appraising stare.

"No charges. I'm letting you go," he sighed, finally, shaking his head.

"But I thought . . ."

"I *said* it depended on how the questioning went! Well, I just can't believe you'd be stupid enough to get involved in this smuggling thing knowingly. If you had, you'd have protected yourself better than you did. What you did was dumb . . . but just dumb enough to ring true."

"Gee, thanks, Captain. I . . ."

"No thanks necessary. Just doing my job. Now get outta here . . . and Mister Skeeve?"

"I know," I smiled, "don't change hotels or leave the dimension without . . ."

"Actually," the captain said drily without a trace of warmth in his voice. "I was going to suggest the exact opposite . . . that you leave the dimension . . . say, by tomorrow morning?"

"What?"

"I still think you smell of trouble, and these reports confirm it. The smuggling thing just seems like too much small potatoes for you to bother with. I'd rather see you gone than put you in jail on a piddling charge like that . . . but it's going to be one or the other, get me?"

I couldn't believe it! Perv was the nastiest, roughest dimension around and *I* was being thrown off as an undesirable!!

Chapter Twenty:

"Were you looking for me?"
— Dr. Livingstone

I was surprised to find Pookie waiting for me when I got back to the hotel. The police had been nice enough to wait until I had given her her check before hauling me off, so I had thought I'd never see her again.

"Hello, Pookie. What brings you here?"

"I wanted to talk a little business with you," she said. "It didn't seem the right time before, so I waited."

"I see."

After my last experience, I wasn't wild about the idea of doing business with Pervects . . . especially ones who didn't want to talk in front of the police. Still, Pookie had given me no reason to distrust her.

"Okay. Come on upstairs and say what's on your mind. It seems I'm leaving . . . on request."

If my statement seemed at all strange to her, she never let on. Instead, she fell in step with me as I entered the hotel.

"Actually, what I have to say shouldn't take too long. If I understand correctly, you're on your way off-dimension

191

to rejoin your regular crew in a campaign against someone named Queen Hemlock. Right?''

"That's a fair summation," I nodded. "Why?"

"I thought I'd offer my services to you for the upcoming brawl. I can give you a special discount for work away from Perv because off-dimension prices are lower. That keeps my overhead down.''

She flashed me a smile that was gone almost as soon as it appeared.

For some reason, it had never occurred to me to hire her for the Hemlock campaign. Still, the idea had merit.

"I don't know, Pookie," I said, trying to weigh the pluses and minuses without taking too much time. "I've already got a couple of bodyguards waiting for me."

"I know," she nodded. "I can do more than bodyguard, and from the sound of the odds you can probably use a little extra help."

"I can use a *lot* of help!" I admitted.

"Well, even though you couldn't find your friend, it does show that you and yours don't mind working with Pervects. Besides, I can travel the dimensions well enough to get us to Klah directly."

That settled it. I had been unsure that my plan to simply remove my monitor ring would be an effective way to signal Massha for a pickup, and Pookie had just come up with a good way to get there. Whatever Massha was doing right now, I wasn't wild about her dropping everything just to provide me with transport.

"All right. You've got yourself a job," I announced. "Just give me a minute to get things together and we'll be off."

That was my original plan, but as I opened the door to my room, I realized I had a visitor.

"Well, don't just stand there with your mouth open. Are you coming or going?"

If there was any doubt in my mind as to who my visitor was, that greeting banished it.

"AAHZ!"

After all my searching—and soul-searching—I couldn't believe my mentor, friend, and partner was finally in front of my eyes, but there he was!

"That's right. I heard you wanted to talk to me . . . so talk."

"I suppose it's reassuring to know that some things never change, Aahzmandius . . . like you."

That last came from Pookie as she slipped past me into the room.

"Pookie!? Is that you?"

For the moment, Aahz seemed to be as dumbstruck as I was.

"You two know each other?"

Surprised and off-stride, I returned to familiar patterns and asked a redundant question.

"Know each other?" Aahz laughed. "Are you kidding? We're cousins!"

"Distant cousins," Pookie corrected without enthusiasm.

"Really? Why didn't you say anything, Pookie?"

"You never asked."

"But . . . you knew I was looking for him!"

"Actually, it took me a while to put it together, and when I did, I didn't know where he was either. Besides, to tell you the truth, from what I recall, I figured you'd be better off without him."

"Well, well. Little Pookie! Still have the razor tongue, I see."

"Not so little any more, Aahzmandius," the bodyguard

said, a dangerous note creeping into her voice. "Try me sometime and you'll see."

It was clear the two of them weren't on the best of terms. I felt it best to intercede before things got ugly.

"How did you get into my room?"

"Bribed the bellhop," my old partner said, returning his attention to me. "Those guys would sell the key to their mother's store if there was a big enough tip in it for them."

An awkward silence followed. Desperately, I cast about for something to say.

"So how have you been, Aahz?" I ventured, realizing how lame it sounded. "You look great."

"Oh, I've been swell . . . just swell," he spat. "As a matter of fact, it's a good thing I saw your ad in the personals when I did. I was about to head off-dimension. I had forgotten how high the prices are around here."

I made a mental note to pay off the bellhop. It looked like his idea of placing an ad had paid off better than all my running around.

"You can say that again," I agreed. "I sure got ambushed by the cost. Of course, I've never been here before, so I couldn't know . . ."

I broke off, realizing he was staring at me.

"Which brings us back to my original question, Skeeve. What are you doing here and why do you want to talk to me?"

My moment had come, and if Aahz's mood was any indication, I had better make my first pitch good. I probably wouldn't get a second chance. Everything I had considered saying to him the next time we met face to face whirled through my head like a kaleidoscope, mixing randomly with my recent thoughts regarding myself.

My search had given me new insight into Aahz. Seeing

the dimension that spawned and shaped him, having learned about his schooldays, and having met his mother, I had a much clearer picture of what made my old partner tick. While I was ready to use that information, I resolved never to let him know how much I had learned. Someday, when he was ready, he might share some of it with me voluntarily, but until then I felt it was best to let him think his privacy was still unbroached. Of course, that still left me groping for what to say here and now. Should I beg him to come back with me? Should I play on our friendship . . . or use the campaign against Queen Hemlock to lure him back for just one more job?

Suddenly, Kalvin's advice came back to me. There was no right or wrong thing to say. All I could do was try, and hope that it was good enough to reach my alienated friend. If not . . .

Taking a deep breath, I gave it my best shot.

"Mostly, I came to apologize, Aahz."

"Apologize?"

My words seemed to startle him.

"That's right. I treated you rather shabbily . . . back before you left. I've got no right to ask you to come back, but I did want to find you to offer my apology and an explanation, for what it's worth. You see . . ."

Now that I had started, my words poured out in a rush, popping out without conscious thought on my part.

"I was so afraid in my new position as head of M.Y.T.H. Inc. that I went overboard trying to live up to what I thought everybody expected of me. I tried to cover up my own weaknesses . . . to appear strong, by doing everything without any help from anybody. I wouldn't even accept the same help that had been given to me before I accepted the position, and either ignored or snapped at any offers of advice or assistance because I saw them as admissions of my own shortcomings.''

I looked at him steadily.

"It was a dumb, immature, jackass way to act, but worst of all it hurt my friends because it made them feel useless and unwanted. That was bad enough for Tananda and Chumley and the others, and I'll be apologizing to them, too, but it was an unforgivable way to treat you."

Licking my lips, I went for it.

"I've never been all that good with words, Aahz, and I doubt I'll ever be able to tell you how much you mean to me. I said I couldn't ask you to come back, and I won't, but I will say that if you do come back, you'll be more than welcome. I'd like a chance to show you what I can't find the words to say . . . that I admire you and value the wisdom and guidance you've always given me. I can't promise that I'll be able to change completely or immediately, but I'm going to try . . . whether you come back or not. I *do* know it'll be easier if you're there to box my ears when I start to slip. I wish . . . well, that's all. It doesn't start to even things out, but you've got my apology."

I lapsed into silence, waiting for his response.

"You know, Skeeve, you're growing up. I think we both forget that more often than we should."

Aahz's voice was so soft I barely recognized it as his.

"Does this mean you'll come back?"

"I . . . I'll have to think about it." he said, looking away. "Let me get back to you in a couple of days. Okay?"

"I'd like to, but I can't," I grimaced. "I've got to leave tonight."

"I see," Aahz's head snapped around. "You could only allow so much time for this little jaunt, huh? Work piling up back at the office?"

An angry, indignant protest rose to my lips, but I fought

back. From what he knew, Aahz's assumption wasn't only not out of line, it was a logical error.

"That's not it at all," I said quietly. "If you must know, the local police have told me to be off-dimension by morning."

"What!!?? You've been tossed off Perv?"

My old partner's eyes fixed on Pookie with cold fury.

"What have you two been up to that could get you tossed off a dimension like this?"

"Don't look at me, cousin! This is the first I've heard of it. The last thing I knew he was heading off-dimension because he couldn't find you."

"That was before my last interview with the police," I supplied. "Really, Aahz, Pookie had nothing to do with it. It's a little mess I got into on my own over . . . the details aren't really important right now. The bottom line is that I can't hang around while you make up your mind."

"Well someday I want to hear those 'unimportant details,' " Aahz growled. "In the meantime, I suppose you can go on ahead and I'll catch up with you after I've thought things out."

"Um . . . actually, if you decide to come, I'll be over on Klah, not Deva."

I tried to make it sound casual, but Aahz caught it in a flash.

"Klah? What would take you back to that backwater dimension?"

There was no way around the direct question. Besides, my old mentor's tone of voice called for a no-nonsense answer.

"Well, there's a problem I've got to deal with there. Remember Queen Hemlock? It seems she's on the move again."

"Hemlock?" Aahz frowned. "I thought you cooled her

jets with a ring that wouldn't come off.''

I decided it wasn't the time to ask what a jet was.

"I did," I acknowledged. "She sent it back to me . . . finger and all. It looked like a pretty clear announcement and a warning that she was all set to launch her world conquest plans again . . . and wasn't about to put up with any interference.''

" . . . And you're about to go up against her alone? Without even mentioning it to me?''

"I . . . I didn't think it would be fair to try to pressure you with it, Aahz. Face it, the way things seem to go there will always be some kind of trouble cropping up. You can't be expected to spend your life covering my tail every time I get in a scrape. Besides, I'm not going to try to take her on myself. In fact, the rest of the team is already there. I sent them on ahead while I came back to look for you.''

I was expecting an explosion and a lecture. Instead, Aahz seemed to be studying my face.

"Let me see if I've got this right," he said, finally. "Your home dimension is under attack . . . and instead of leading the team in the campaign, you put it all on hold to come looking for me?''

When he put it that way, it *did* sound more than a little irresponsible.

"Well . . . yes," I stammered. "But I told Massha to come pick me up at the end of a week. I figured that I'd have to go and pitch in at that point, whether I had found you or not.''

Aahz started to say something, then shook his head. Heaving a great sigh, he tried again.

"Skeeve . . . don't worry about not being able to find the right words. I think you've given me a pretty good idea of what I really mean to you.''

"I did?"

He nodded.

"Enough that I've decided I don't need any more time to make up my mind. Grab your stuff, partner. Let's get going. Are you square with the hotel, or do you still have to settle accounts?"

"I'm all set on that front," I said. "There's no balance . . . since they made me pay in advance."

"That figures," Aahz grumbled. "Unless you're a VIP or something, everybody gets the same treatment."

It was just too good an opening to pass up, and I yielded to the temptation.

"Of course, it'll probably be easier for me next time around . . . now that I have a line of credit and a credit card."

"What next time around? I thought you said the police . . ."

His train of thought stopped abruptly as he turned to loom over me.

"CREDIT CARD? What credit card? Who's been teaching you about credit cards?"

That wasn't exactly the reaction I had been expecting.

"The bank suggested it, actually," I explained. "They said . . ."

"What bank? How did you know what to look for in a bank?"

"Well, it was recommended to me by Edvick, he's the cabbie I hired while I was here, and . . ."

"That you hired? Why didn't you . . ." He paused and seemed to regain a bit of control. "It sounds like you've got quite a bit to discuss with me . . . when we have the time. Right, *partner*?"

"Right, Aahz," I said, glad to be off the hook for the moment.

"Is there anything that has to be done *before* we leave?"

"Well, I've got to get some money to the bellhop. I promised him . . ."

"Spare me the details . . . for the moment anyway. Anything else?"

"No, Aahz."

"All right. Finish packing while I hunt up this bellhop for you. Then, we're off for Klah . . . if I can find the settings on the D-hopper, that is. It's been a while, and . . ."

"Save the batteries, cousin," Pookie said. "I think I can handle getting us all there without help."

"You? Since when were you coming along?" Aahz gaped.

"Since I hired on with Skeeve here," the bodyguard countered. "While we're on the subject, since when did you need a D-hopper to travel through the dimensions?"

"Um . . . if the two of you don't mind," I said, stuffing my dirty clothes into my new bag, "could we save all that until later? Right now, we've got a war to catch!"

Magikal mirth'n mayhem from the creator of Thieves' World™

Make no mythstake, this is the wildest, wackiest, most frolicking fantasy series around. With the mythfit Skeeve and his magical mythadventures, Aahz the pervert demon, Gleep the baby dragon, and a crazy cast of mythstifying characters, Robert Asprin's "Myth" series is a guaranteed good time. Join the world of deveels, dragons and magik—and join the wacky adventures of fantasy's most fun-loving mythfits.

BESTSELLING
Science Fiction
and
Fantasy